The Secret Signal

Copyright ©Simon Haynes

Book one in the Hal Junior series

Simon Haynes

Bowman Press

The Hal Junior Series:

The Secret Signal
The Missing Case
The Gyris Mission
The Comet Caper

Simon Haynes also writes the
Hal Spacejock series for teens & adults

... AND the
Harriet Walsh series for teens & adults.

www.spacejock.com.au

Dedicated to all my nieces and nephews

There once was a lad called Hal Junior
Who was gifted a plant by Aunt Lunia
The best thing for me
said Hal earnestly
Is a spaceship and not a petunia!

The Test Flight

'Whoosh! Zoom! Fizz, fizz, *fizz!*' Hal Junior swept his arm through the air, fluttering the wings of a paper plane gripped in his hand.

Laser beams zinged Captain Spacejock's fighter, the Phantom X1, spitting and crackling as they bounced off the hull. The enemy ship was right on his tail, and there was only one way out!

The paper plane swooped, and Hal Junior supplied the sound effects for his epic space battle. 'Vroom! Neeee-ouuw!'

The X1 climbed into the sky, turned on its tail and dived on the pursuer. Catching the enemy ship by surprise, Captain Spacejock fired a burst from his triple-decker space-cannon.

'Dakka dakka dakka! Fizz-fizz-BOOM! Take that, evil minion! You're no match for Captain Spacejock!'

The X1 did a victory roll over the crash site, and then the captain turned for home. Suddenly, an angry voice crackled in his headphones.

'Will you hurry up! We'll be late for lessons!'

Hal lowered the paper plane. Stephen 'Stinky' Binn was a good friend, but Hal sometimes wished he was a robot so he could switch his voice off. 'Stinky! I was on patrol!'

'If you don't quit dreaming you'll be on detention.'

They hurried along the corridor together, with Hal still fighting imaginary space battles. 'Zooom! Zzing! Ker-pow! Aaargh!'

Stinky rolled his eyes.

A lift carried them to the next level, and on the way up Hal showed off his paper plane. His dad had found the diagram in an old ebook the night before, and after demonstrating the basics he'd left Hal to it. His dad was good like that - always there to lend a hand, but never trying to take over and do everything for you.

The plane had come out really well, but it wasn't finished until bed time and their quarters were too small for a test flight. Hal had been pretending to fly it all morning, but it wasn't enough. He was itching to try it for real.

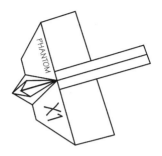

'Teacher's not going to like it,' warned Stinky, gesturing at the plane. 'You were supposed to write your answers on it, not crease it into little squares.'

'Oh yeah?' Hal turned the plane over to reveal several lines of uneven handwriting. 'Shame you're not as smart as me.'

Stinky shook his head. 'You're still going to cop it. That stuff is really precious.'

The class theme for the week was ancient technology, and each student had been given a sheet of paper and a pencil stub for their homework. Paper was scarce aboard the space station, where everything had to be flown in at huge expense.

Hal figured the sheet was going to be recycled anyway, so why not make a plane out of it?

The lift doors opened and Hal launched the plane with a sudden flick of the wrist, almost hitting Stinky in the back of the head. At first it flew beautifully, sailing past doorways and weaving through pipes and struts as though Captain

Spacejock were at the controls. Then ... *whoosh!* A recycling hatch opened with its distinctive sucking noise.

According to Hal's dad the rushing air was supposed to keep nasty smells in, but there were rumours of a giant space monster at the bottom of the shaft. It was supposed to live on scraps of metal and old food, and every time a hatch opened the monster took a gigantic breath, gulping down air to fill its leathery lungs.

Unfortunately, the whooshing air sucked the plane straight into the hatch. Fortunately, when Hal looked inside he found the plane stuck to the damp wall. Unfortunately it was just out of reach.

— 2 —

A 'Rappelling' Idea

'Come on, you stubborn slice of tree pulp!' Hal's arms were at full stretch, but his grasping fingers couldn't quite reach the paper plane stuck to the grimy metal wall.

'Have you got it yet?'

'What do you think?' snapped Hal, twisting his neck to give Stinky an upside-down glare.

'I think I can't hold on much longer.'

Unfortunately Stinky wasn't talking about his frequent trips to the bathroom. No, Stinky was braced against the recycling hatch, holding Hal by the ankles. His fingers were the only thing saving his friend from a headlong plunge down Space Station Oberon's main recycling chute.

'You can do it,' said Hal. 'Just a bit lower.'

'I can't. You'll have to leave it.'

Leave it . . . leave it . . . leave it! echoed the chute.

Hal grabbed and missed. It was so annoying! He was close enough to read his own writing, but it could have been a light year away for all the use that was. 'Scribbling on paper is a stupid idea. Why couldn't we stick to writing answers in our workbooks?'

'Instead of sticking them to the wall, you mean?' Stinky shifted his grip. 'It's lucky Teacher didn't give us stone tablets to write on.'

'Don't be an idiot. If he'd given us a slab of rock I'd hardly have made a paper plane, would I?'

'No, you'd have lobbed it through a window instead.' Stinky thought for a moment. 'Why don't we share my paper? You can write your answers on the back.'

Hal snorted. He rarely did his homework the first time, and doing it twice was out of the question. Frustrated, he scowled at the paper plane. Any minute now they'd be marked absent, and by the time he finished detention a fresh load of garbage would have brushed his homework straight down the chute. No, it was now or never. 'Hey, I've got a brilliant idea. Let go of my ankles.'

'You call that brilliant?'

'Sure. I'll drop a bit further if you hold my shoes.'

'You'll drop a lot further if they slip off your feet.'

'They wouldn't come off if you shot them with a blast rifle. I used my patented triple knot.'

Stinky knew all about Hal's patented ideas, but nonetheless he shifted his grip to Hal's shoes.

'Just a bit more!' cried Hal, as his outstretched fingers brushed the plane's wing.

'That's all, Hal. I swear.'

'The laces. Hold me by the shoelaces!'

By now Stinky was beyond arguing, and he obeyed despite his misgivings.

Unfortunately, Hal's original laces had been burnt to a crisp in the great model rocket affair. Fortunately his dad had replaced them. Unfortunately he'd used elastic.

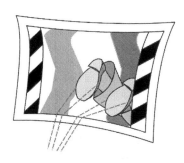

Hal went down the chute like a bungee-jumping hamster – his arms outstretched and a look of wide-eyed shock on his face. The weight almost pulled

Stinky through the hatch, but he just managed to brace himself.

Boinnnnggg!

Stretched to capacity, the elastic contracted, yanking Hal backwards up the chute. For a split second he was face to face with Stinky, and he couldn't help laughing at his friend's startled upside-down expression.

Whoosh!

Gravity reasserted itself, and Hal went back down the chute. This time he stuck his hand out, and with a triumphant yell he peeled the plane from the wall. 'I've got it, Stinky. I've got it!'

Boinnnnggg!

Hal didn't bounce as far this time, or the next, and after bobbing up and down a few more times he finally came to rest, turning slowly in mid-air as he dangled by his extremely long shoelaces. 'I told you it would work. Now get me out of here.'

Stinky pulled, but Hal didn't move.

'Go on. Put some effort into it!'

'I can't!' said Stinky in alarm. 'Hal, you're too heavy. I can't pull you up!'

A 'Repelling' Idea

Hal's blood froze as he realised the danger he was in. Stinky couldn't hold on forever, and if Hal stayed in the chute much longer he was going to fall all the way to the bottom. 'Don't mess about. Pull me up!'

'I can't do it on my own. You'll have to help.'

Muttering under his breath, Hal took the paper plane between his teeth and pressed his palms against the smooth metal walls. He tried to push himself back up the tunnel, but his hands just slipped. Meanwhile, Stinky was hauling on the springy shoelaces with all his might. 'It's no use. It's not working. And Hal . . . I've got to go.'

Go . . . go . . . go!

Hal looked puzzled. 'We've both got to go, Stinky. That's the problem . . . I'm stuck.'

'No, I mean go!' said Stinky, and this time he was

talking about his frequent trips to the bathroom.

'Just hold it in, all right?' Hal thought furiously. If he couldn't climb up to safety, what about going down instead? He squinted into the shadowy depths and saw an access hatch one level down. If Stinky let go of his laces, could he grab the hatch as he flew past? If not that one, maybe the one after? The problem was, once he started falling he'd move faster and faster and then nothing would stop him until he went SPLAT at the very bottom of the space station. If he didn't end up like a pancake he'd probably starve before anyone found him. Unless there really was a space monster down there, in which case it'd be one gulp and goodnight.

Teacher A Space Monster?

'I have an idea,' called Stinky, his voice echoing off the slick metal walls. 'If I reverse the gravity in the chute it'll push you back up instead of pulling you down.'

'Do you think it'll do the trick?'

'Reversing the polarity always works.'

'Cool. Give it a shot.' That was the best thing about Stinky – he wasn't much good at hauling people out of garbage hatches by their shoelaces, but he was a whizz with electronics.

'You'll have to hang on. I need both hands.'

'I'm not going anywhere,' said Hal, praying he was right. His shoes went slack as Stinky let go of the laces, and he braced himself against the sides of the tunnel. Before long his arms started to ache, and then he had a worrying thought. What if someone a few levels up decided to recycle a coffee pot, or a dirty nappy, or even a fridge? That would really cap his day off. 'Will you hurry up?' he shouted. 'I'm starting to slip!'

Slip! Slip! Slip!

There was a crackle near his feet and a cloud of blue smoke wafted by. All of a sudden Hal was weightless, and he was just flexing his sore arms when the world turned upside-down. Suddenly he was standing upright . . . on thin air.

With a surprised 'whoof' Hal shot upwards like a human cannonball in the world's biggest and most dangerous circus act. Far below, there was a rumble and a clatter as all the junk in the recycling plant rose towards the roof of the station.

Hal grabbed the edge of the hatch as he fell past, and he was still struggling to climb out when he saw the mass of twisted junk hurtling up the shaft like a runaway train. Imagine a kitchen bin firing banana skins and eggshells and yesterday's lunch all over the roof – then imagine standing over the bin and looking into it as the contents flew out. That's what Hal was facing. But it wasn't yucky food scraps he was worried about, it was old computers, tatty furniture and leftover building materials. The shaft was like the barrel of a gun, the fast-moving junk was the bullet and Hal was a bug about to get squished.

The mass was moving incredibly fast, and it pushed the air ahead of it in a howling gale. Hatches banged and clattered in the shaft, and all over the station people gasped, spluttered and fainted as a foul-smelling hurricane blew through their offices, kitchens and lounge rooms.

With an effort, Hal tore his gaze from the impending doom. 'Help! Stinky!'

Stinky … stinky … stinky!

His friend dragged him out of the hatch with seconds to spare. Hal landed in the corridor and there was a tremendous clatter as the junk flew past. By the time he recovered Stinky was busy at the control panel.

'What's going to happen when that lot hits the roof?' demanded Hal.

'It's going to smash right through,' said Stinky, who was picking through a tangle of wires. 'There's a safety seal to keep the air in, but the damage will be insane.'

'You've got to stop it. Quick!'

'What do you think I'm doing?'

There was a crackle from the control panel, a moment of total silence, and then all the junk turned round and plummeted towards the base of the station. The inhabitants were only just recovering from the first gale, having straightened their pictures and combed the scraps of muck out of their hair. Now they got a second dose.

With hatches clattering up and down the shaft, and the mass of junk safely back in the recycling centre, Stinky finished his work and jammed the cover back on the panel. After a hurried look around to make sure they hadn't left any evidence, the two boys ran for it.

'I've got to change my jumper,' said Stinky, whose sleeves were smeared with grime from the hatch. It wasn't just his sleeves - his hair looked like it had been dipped in a rubbish bin and blow-dried in a wind tunnel. Hal looked even worse . . . but that was normal.

'See you in class, Stinky. And thanks!'

Stinky hurried off to his family's living quarters, while Hal slowed to a walk. In his experience, running anywhere on the station led to awkward questions like 'Where have you been?', 'Where are you going?' and worst of all, 'Did you just blow all my paintings off the wall and what's this piece of orange peel doing in my hair?'

As he walked along the corridor Hal heard the familiar rush and gurgle of liquid in the overhead pipes. His dad said the noise was the station's lifeblood pumping through its arteries and veins, but Hal suspected this was a load of sewage.

He slowed as he approached a set of doors marked 'Observation Deck'. Was there time for a quick look at the stars?

Of course there was!

— 4 —

Off Limits

Of all the cool places aboard Space Station Oberon, the observation deck was Hal's favourite. He loved to stand with his nose flattened against the big perspex window, his eyes drinking in the distant stars. When he cupped his hands to his face, shutting out the reflections, he could pretend he was floating in space like the repair crews with their spacesuits and jet packs. What he wouldn't give to go flying around the Oberon in a powered suit! Imagine the races they could have! Playing awesome games of tag, weaving through the docking ports, zipping past the living quarters and the connecting tunnels . . .

Hal sighed, knowing it could never happen. Adults took all the fun out of everything, and even the exciting-sounding spacesuit training was just putting on the same sweaty old overalls while someone shouted 'faster, faster!' in your ear.

In the distance, almost lost in the vast starfield, there was a yellowish patch of light. Hal's teacher had once pointed it out as a habitable system, and to Hal that meant planets and oceans and memories of playing outdoors. He remembered a grassy field, the warm sun beating down on him, the feel of the breeze and the chirrups and squawks of insects and birds. He'd only been three or four years old, but he still remembered the oozy squishy mud between his fingers. No mud on a space station, that was for sure. No sunlight or insects either, nor grassy fields.

Hal sighed and shifted his gaze to an area of the starfield above and to his left, seeking out an oval patch of light. Teacher had told him the name of the galaxy once, but Hal called it The Snot because it looked like the time Stinky Binn had sneezed inside his space helmet.

'All students from D-Section please report to pod three for lessons. I repeat, all students report to pod three immediately.'

Hal glanced at his watch, an impressive-looking timepiece he'd found in a pile of construction junk. The adult-sized watch was huge on his wrist, and the chunky strap was so loose he didn't have to undo it to take it off. The dial looked like it might have been used in space, and the buttons had mysterious legends like O_2 and TMI.

In class he always rolled his sleeve up so everyone could marvel at his treasure. The only problem was that he couldn't tell the time with it, because it didn't work. He'd tried levering the back off to swap the battery, but it needed a special tool. He couldn't ask an adult in case they took his precious watch away.

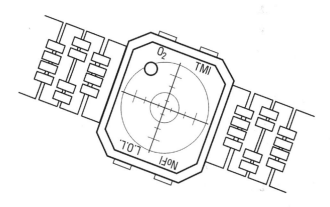

'I repeat, ALL students please report to pod three for lessons. That includes you, Hal Junior!'

Hal smoothed the paper plane and slipped it into the tough plastic case of his workbook. He'd spent almost three minutes working on the answers the night before, and for once they'd been easy. In fact, he was looking forward to handing it in, which is why he'd gone to so much trouble saving his plane from the recycling shaft.

He was about to leave when the doors slid open, and his heart sank as he saw the dumpy figure outside. It was the station's head of security, Grant Bignew, his thinning hair all messed up and his eyes bulging like a toad's. 'What are you doing here, boy? Don't you know this area is off limits? Why, I could have you thrown in jail!'

Hal and Stinky called the chief 'Giant Bignose' behind his back, but this wasn't the time to bring that up. Instead, Hal put on his best manner. 'Please sir, I'm very sorry. I thought I heard a noise, but when I came in to investigate there was nobody here.'

'Is that so?' Bignew studied Hal intently. 'I can always tell when people are lying, boy. Are you lying to me?'

'No sir, definitely not.'

'Excellent. Now run along and don't let me catch you in here again!'

Hal fled, relieved he wasn't in handcuffs. A few weeks earlier Hal's dad let another worker use his supervisor code so they could finish an urgent repair on time. This 'crime' had led to a public telling-off by Bignew. After that, Hal's dad referred to the head of security as 'that officious little toad', at least until

Hal's mother pointed out their apartment could be bugged.

As he hurried along the corridor Hal wondered what Bignose was doing in the observation deck. Did he use high-powered binoculars to spy on the rest of the station? Was there a secret door leading to a hidden lair? Hal snorted at the crazy idea. Bignose probably liked the stars.

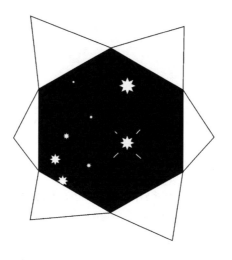

— 5 —

Teach and Spell

By the time Hal got to class the lesson was in full swing. There were two dozen children sitting at folding desks while Teacher sped around the room collecting assignments. Their Teacher was an old-style robot with a red plastic body and short stubby arms. The words 'Teach and Spell' were printed across his chest in big yellow letters, and instead of a face he had a large screen which could display up to a dozen eyes at once. These eyes could move independently, squinting or winking or glaring at several different students all at the same time. They weren't limited to the front either: when Teacher turned to project lessons onto the classroom wall, a stray eye would sometimes appear round the back of his head, checking up on the students. There was one particularly busy eye which Hal called 'the follower', because no matter where he sat it always seemed to follow him around the room.

Teacher rolled past Hal on his silent rubber wheels, whisking the paper plane out of his fingers. 'Thank you for putting in an appearance, Hal Junior. Please have a seat.'

Hal took an empty desk alongside Stinky, while Teacher rolled to the front of the room and turned to face the students. 'Today we're going to discuss obsolete communications methods, including semaphore, Morse code and email. But first, I shall mark your chemistry homework.' He held up the assignments and flipped through them, faster than the eye could see. Then he looked around the class. 'Good efforts, everyone. And I see one student handed in something rather special.' Teacher held up the paper plane between finger and thumb. 'Hal Junior, you really went to town on presentation.'

Hal grinned. No more bottom of the class for him!

Teacher unfolded the plane to read Hal's answers, his eyes squinting and flickering as he struggled with the handwriting. When he was done he peered at Hal over the top of the assignment. 'Hal Junior, I'm going to read out your replies out so the entire class can marvel at them. Question one: Name three heavy metals. Your answer: thrash, power and drone.'

Hal smiled confidently at the other students, basking in their puzzled looks. He'd spent several minutes researching the answers, and the online encyclopaedia was never wrong. There were pages and pages of information on heavy metal, along with pictures of guitars and drum kits. Hal had even drawn a few in the margins, and he was particularly proud of the big skull with gleaming diamonds for teeth.

'Question two: Describe the reaction when you add sodium chloride to water.' Teacher looked at him over the top of the paper. 'Your answer: It gets wet.'

Hal nodded. The solution was so obvious he hadn't even looked it up. There were a few gasps around him, and he realised some of them hadn't been able to answer the question. That was their problem . . . they should have come to him for help.

'Finally, question three: Name the heaviest element on the periodic table. Your answer, Mr Junior, was 'thickonium'.'

The class erupted in laughter, and Hal frowned. What was wrong with them?

Even Teacher's digital lips creased into a grin. 'Mr Junior, a few months ago you said your goal was to become a space pilot. With these results, I guarantee the only space you'll navigate is the one between your ears. Unless, of course, your head is packed with thickonium!'

The class laughed even harder at this, and Hal slid down in his chair, his face burning. He'd asked his best mate for help, and this is what he got? To his credit Stinky was trying not to laugh, but his face had turned red from the effort.

Right, thought Hal. If this was the praise he got for doing his homework, Teacher could whistle for it in future.

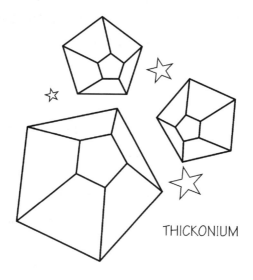

THICKONIUM

'Okay class, settle down. I mentioned obsolete communications earlier. Can anyone tell me what obsolete means?'

Every hand reached for the sky, and Hal slowly raised his own to match. He had no idea what the word meant, but he wasn't going to let on.

'Hal Junior, you seem uncertain. Perhaps you could share your definition with the rest of us?'

Oh, great. Why did Teacher have to single him out? Hal lowered his hand, thinking furiously. Then his face cleared as he remembered his parents using the word in a recent conversation. 'Obsolete means when you're really fat.'

There were hoots of laughter from the rest of the class, and Teacher motioned for silence. 'Can anyone correct Mr Junior here?'

All the hands went up again, waving like stalks of sea-grass in the hydroponics lab.

'Natalie?'

'Obsolete means old and no longer useful.'

'Just like Teacher,' muttered Hal.

The class gasped at the remark, but Teacher pretended not to hear. 'And the word Mr Junior defined for us? Can anyone tell me what the correct term is?'

Natalie shook her head, and Hal grinned. Take that, little miss smarty-pants.

'Anyone?' Teacher's electronic eyes darted all over his face as he scanned the class, but this time nobody raised a hand. 'Very well. The word

Mr Junior described was 'obesity', and you can research the topic for homework.'

The class groaned, and several students shot accusing looks at Hal. He returned each one with his patented one-eyed scowl.

'Don't worry, half a page on the subject will be plenty. Now let me spell it for you.' Teacher gave them the letters one by one, then looked around the class. 'Tell me, does anyone know what a semaphore is?'

This time Hal was ready. Teacher was picking on anyone who looked unsure, so he stuck his hand up immediately. Unfortunately, his was the only hand in the air.

'Mr Junior, you're full of surprises today. Please, will you share your knowledge with the class?'

Hal thought hard. Semaphore sounded like carnivore, and he knew what that was because they'd studied lions and tigers recently. And the other part of the word? Semi meant half – he remembered that from a song about bees. So what was something which only ate half the meat? Then it came to him. 'Dieters!'

'I'm sorry?'

'People on a diet are semaphores. They only eat half their food.'

Teacher blinked once or twice. He was

programmed to handle most situations but even he had his limits. 'We're discussing obsolete communications such as Morse code and email, and you think this has something to do with dieting?'

Hal put his hand up. 'Would you like me to explain Morse?'

'Please don't,' said Teacher.

Sensing a weakness, Hal decided to try. Morse sounded like . . . well, horse. And it started with an M, which meant millions. Easy! 'Morse is a very big herd of ponies.'

Some of Teacher's eyes started to spin in circles, while others bounced off the top and bottom of his screen as though someone were playing a computer game with his face.

'How about email? I bet I could explain that.'

'Please don't. There's no need.'

There was no stopping Hal now. Mail was the opposite of female, and E meant energy. 'Email is a sportsman.'

'No no NO!' All of teacher's eyes stopped at once, some pointing at the ceiling, some at the floor, and only one on Hal. Unfortunately it was the follower, and it didn't look happy. 'Hal Junior. Please do not raise your hand again.'

'What if I have a question sir?'

'Then you may raise your hand.'

Hal immediately put his hand up.

'Y-yes?'

'Sir, what is a semaphore?'

'It's a signalling system involving flags. The sender waves flags in patterns, and the receiver looks up the patterns in a book to decode the message.'

Hal's hand shot up.

'What now?'

'How do you send a message if the other guy doesn't have a copy of the book?'

'You don't, which is why Morse is superior.' Teacher played several long beeps followed by several short ones. 'Do you hear the difference?'

Everyone nodded.

'You can transmit Morse using flashes of light, bursts of sound ... even vibrations. Now, we're almost out of time so I'll cover email in tomorrow's lesson. For homework I want the essay on obesity and I want you to write your own names using Morse code. I've uploaded a copy of the alphabet so you can perform a simple letter substitution.'

Hal frowned. It might be simple for Teacher but he'd wrestle with it for ages. On the plus side, he could wait until his parents tried to pack him off to bed and then tell them he had urgent homework to do. With a bit of luck they'd finish it off for him.

Then it hit him – Morse was a secret code! He could send messages by tapping on the desk! Flash messages to other sections through the observation window!

Excited, Hal opened his workbook and blew a fine layer of dust off the screen. The device powered up slowly, and a progress bar crawled across the screen as several weeks' worth of lessons, assignment questions and updates were installed. When it was finally ready Hal turned to the Morse alphabet. There it was – dots, dashes and letters – a secret code just waiting to be used. Hal barely noticed the other kids leaving the classroom, and he only looked up when Teacher came over.

'Hal Junior, this room is required for spacesuit training. You must leave now.'

'Sorry sir. On my way.' Hal pushed his chair back and left, almost bumping into a group of scientists filing into the room. They were grumbling about sweaty overalls and people shouting 'faster, faster' in their ears, but Hal didn't stop to listen. He had some learning to do!

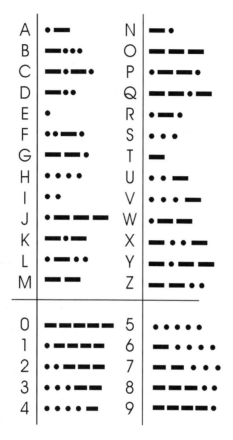

Morse Code

— 6 —

Two Suspects

'I'm sorry about that thickonium business,' said Stinky. 'I thought you realised I was joking.'

Hal snorted. 'Some friend you are, setting me up like that. Were you trying to get me in trouble?'

'I didn't think you'd write it down!' Stinky shot Hal a sidelong glance. 'Anyway, if you'd looked up the answer like you were supposed to . . .'

Stinky's voice tailed off as they rounded the corner and almost walked into a maintenance worker. The fair-haired woman was standing near the recycling hatch Hal had climbed into earlier, frowning at a diagnostic screen. Nearby, the cover was off the control panel, exposing the innards.

'Act normal,' muttered Hal. 'Don't say anything!'

They walked past, pretending to study the opposite wall, the ceiling and the floor – trying to look anywhere but the exposed control panel – but it didn't work.

'Hold up, lads. Did you two see anyone around here earlier?'

'N-no Miss, not us. Nobody at all.'

The woman glanced at Stinky. 'What about you?' she demanded. 'Have you seen anyone acting suspiciously?'

Hal prayed his friend would keep his mouth shut, and he was relieved when Stinky studied his shoes and said nothing.

'Meddling with these systems is a very serious matter.' The woman handed Hal a card. 'If you see anyone poking around in the control box I want you to get in touch immediately.'

'Yes Ma'am.' Hal studied the card and discovered the woman was Tina Peters, trainee maintenance officer. She didn't look like she was about to throw them both in the nearest cell, but then again she didn't know it was Stinky who'd almost blown the roof off the space station.

Tina closed the control panel and took out a workpad. It was similar to Hal's workbook except for the dark grey colour and the chrome strips down the side. It looked cool, and Hal thought it was typical how schoolkids got the daggy brown ones with fake wood-grain. Tina tapped the screen, then frowned. 'This thing's on the blink. Do you have the time by any chance?'

Hal shook his head.

Tina pointed to his watch. 'What's that, a ham sandwich?'

'It doesn't work,' said Hal, shaking his sleeve until it covered the chunky metal band.

'Want me to take a look at it for you?'

'No, it's fine.'

Tina put a hand out. 'Come on, I'll have it working in no time.'

Unwillingly, Hal removed the watch. Tina inspected it, and then before Hal could stop her she swung it at the wall.

CRACK!

'Hey!' shouted Hal. 'What are you doing?'

Tina smiled and held the watch out. To Hal's

surprise, the display now showed a jumble of random letters.

'How did you –?'

'Corrosion in the power circuit. If you let me have it for a couple of days I'll clean the contacts and replace the battery.'

Hal eyed the precious watch. What if he never got it back? 'I'll keep hold of it, if that's all right.'

'Are you sure? It's no good like this.' Tina turned the watch over. 'This is a genuine space watch. Did your parents give it to you?'

'Someone left it to me,' said Hal, who never lied if he could bend the truth.

'Very generous of them. These things can do everything.'

'Really? Like what?'

'It'll talk to your spacesuit and tell you when your air is getting low. It'll tell you whether it's safe to take your helmet off, and it has a built-in homing beacon. Configure it for the space station and it'll always point the way home.' Tina laughed. 'It'll even tell the time, when it's working properly.'

'That's amazing,' said Hal.

Tina thought for a moment. 'Tell you what, you keep an eye out for whoever is messing with this control panel and I'll fix your watch. Deal?'

Hal was tempted, but it wouldn't be right. After all,

it was his fault Tina was investigating the control panel. 'Thanks, but I'll keep it.'

'Fine. If you change your mind, let me know.' Tina took out her workpad. 'What's your name?'

'Hal Junior.'

'And your friend?'

'Stin– I mean, Stephen Binn.'

Tina held the workpad to her mouth. 'Two suspects identified, age approximately ten to twelve. Interview suspended until further notice.'

Hal and Stinky stared at Tina in shock. Was she an undercover cop disguised as an ordinary technician? How much trouble were they in?

The young woman regarded them with a deadly serious face, and Hal was just about to confess everything from the finding of the watch to the episode with the recycling hatch when Tina exploded with laughter. After a moment or two, during which the boys simply stared with their mouths open, she wiped her eyes with her sleeve and took a couple of deep breaths. 'Sorry lads, just a little joke. You should have seen your faces!'

Tina packed the workpad in her toolbox and went on her way, still laughing to herself.

Hal and Stinky exchanged a glance, both clearly thinking the same thing. If someone as loony as

Tina could get a job fixing the space station, the place was about as safe as a cardboard airlock.

SPACE

This SPACE intentionally left blank

Surprise News

Hal touched the access panel outside his family's quarters, and the door opened with a groan. His parents were sitting at the kitchen table, and his mother looked worried. 'The gravity in the shaft reversed without warning. According to Maintenance we were seconds from a major hull breach. It could have wiped out –'

Hal's father shot her a warning glance. 'Have a seat, son.'

Hal squeezed behind the tiny kitchen table and sat on the narrow bench. There was no wasted space in their quarters – even the bench had doors in the front so items could be stashed away out of sight. When he was smaller Hal would climb right inside while his parents pretended to look for him inside their coffee cups and under the salt shaker. They even – shock horror – opened the recycling hatch and called down the chute for him. Eventually his giggling fits would give him away and his parents would make a show of 'finding' him.

Now the space was filled with old kitchen junk.

'Your mum and I have some good news.'

Hal's eyes narrowed. If it was a new baby . . .

'I've been promoted,' said his mum, with a twinkle in her eyes. 'Old Benton is retiring and moving back to Gyris. They've given me his job.'

'Your mother is going to be head of research,' said Hal's dad proudly. His own speciality was the atmosphere scrubbers, where he worked long hours to make sure everyone had clean air to breathe. He liked to tell everyone he was good with his hands while his wife was good with her brains, making the pair of them a great team.

'Do we get any benefits?' asked Hal.

His dad laughed. 'Trust you to think of that.'

'Well?'

'We'll be moving to bigger quarters in C-Section,' said his mum. 'You'll have a terminal in your room, so you'll be able to do your homework on time every night.'

'Wonderful,' muttered Hal. Still, new quarters sounded good and the terminal would be very handy once Stinky performed some of his hacker magic on it. 'Hang on, what about school?'

'They have a modern teacher, much newer than the one you're used to. Just think, you'll meet some new friends too.'

'Have you met the kids from C-Section?' scoffed Hal. 'They think they're a cut above the rest of us. Anyway, Stinky's the only friend I need.'

'Stin– I mean, Stephen can come and visit whenever you like.'

'When are we moving?'

'Benton isn't leaving for a day or so,' explained his mum. 'I'm going to be very busy getting up to speed. I'm afraid that means working longer hours for a bit.'

'You already work long hours.'

'This is very important son,' said his dad. 'Your mum can't give you all the details, but if the research pays off it'll change life for everyone.'

'Even mine and Stinky's?'

His father laughed. 'Yes, yours too.'

◆

Half an hour later Hal stood at the dishwasher,

placing dirty plates and cutlery on the moving belt. As the items emerged from the other end, shiny and clean, he put them away. He'd heard others complaining about 'doing the dishes' but it didn't seem that bad to him. Their machine was old and slow – what was the word Teacher had used? Obsolete, that was it – but it sure beat eating dinner off dirty plates.

Ever impatient, Hal added more and more items to the dishwasher, cramming them in until they barely cleared the intake. The machine chugged and groaned with the extra weight, and when it ground to a complete stop Hal turned to the controls. The dial was fixed on 'Slow', and Hal reckoned his parents left it there to keep him busy after dinner. They'd warned him not to touch it, but surely one little tweak wouldn't hurt?

He reached for the big plastic dial and turned it from 'Slow' to 'Medium'.

Whirrr!

The machine started to move again, and the plates coming out the other end were clean enough. There was a speck of food here and there, but who was going to notice? Hal eyed the pile of cups and cutlery he still had to deal with, and decided to do the whole lot in one go. He put all the items on the belt and twisted the knob through 'Fast', 'Very Fast', 'Very

Very Fast' . . . all the way up to 'Ultra-Fast'

Zooooooooom!

The belt fairly flew as the machine kicked into top speed, and the crockery disappeared into the machine as though sucked into a black hole.

Zzzinngg!

Gleaming cutlery arrowed out of the dishwasher, streaking across the kitchen in a blur of silver.

Gadoiinnnggg! went the knives and forks as they stuck into the wall, quivering with the force.

Spat-spat-spat! went the dishwasher, rocking on its feet as it hurled teacups around the kitchen.

Clatter clatter crash! went the plastic cups and plates as they bounced off the walls and cupboards.

Hal ducked under the barrage and turned the

knob back to 'Slow'. The last plate had just stopped spinning when his dad appeared in the doorway.

'Don't look at me,' said Hal. 'It just went wrong. I think it's . . . obsolete.'

His dad crouched to gather the scattered crockery, shaking his head at the mess. Hal tried to give him a hand, but ended up smearing food scraps all over the floor with the broom.

'It'll be quicker if I do it,' said his dad. 'Go and start your homework.'

Hal nearly reached the exit before his dad called him back to wash his hands. Hal put his hands in the sink and there was a tingly blue glow as the field did its job. When he raised his hands they were perfectly clean and dry. His dad once told him about people washing with actual water, splashing it all over themselves like there was an endless supply. Aboard a space station water was hoarded for drinking, and the idea of pouring it on your skin or sloshing it all over your plates to clean them was insane. In fact, Hal sometimes wondered whether his dad made up half the things he told him. Most of them were certainly crazy enough.

After he'd cleaned up Hal went to his cabin, where a narrow bunk jostled for space with a tiny desk and a fold-out chair. It wasn't much of a room, and Hal wondered what their new place might be like.

A computer terminal of his own would be fantastic, especially if Stinky could hack his way around the usual blocks. Unrestricted terminals had views of the outside, huge libraries of music and video, access to any number of cool games and stacks of other delights. For that, he'd even put up with the kids from C-Section.

Hal sat at the desk and opened his workbook, which still had the Morse alphabet on its screen. In all the excitement of meeting Tina the tech and learning about his mum's new job and their new home, he'd forgotten his plan to study the secret code. He figured he had an hour before his parents sent him to bed, and he decided to spend the time learning Morse.

After a while he'd managed to draw his name using dots and dashes, and then he amused himself by converting swear words into code. It wasn't the same though . . . shouting 'dash dot dot, dot dash, dash dash, dash dot' when you tripped over a stray power cable wasn't really practical. By the time you got to the second 'dot' your face would be firmly planted on the floor.

There was a knock, and Hal turned to see his mum in the doorway. 'I'm just doing my homework.'

'Teacher's still fond of Morse code, eh?'

'You know about it?'

'Everyone has to learn Morse. It's very useful.'

Hal's face fell. So much for the secret code. Then he realised his mum was eyeing the workbook screen, where he'd written several choice phrases in Morse. He closed the lid quickly, hoping she hadn't read them.

'I'm glad you've finished. It's time for bed.'

'But I have to do an assignment on obesity!'

His mum raised her eyebrows. 'Hal Junior, you're not pulling that old trick on me. You've had plenty of time to finish your homework.'

'You want me to do well at school, don't you?'

'All right, you can have five minutes.'

'Mum!'

His mum tapped on the door frame: Dash dot, dash, dot. 'And not a second longer.'

Ten minutes later he said goodnight to his parents, turned off the light and clambered into his bunk. In the dark the space station rumbled and thumped and creaked, making all the noises you never heard when the lights were on. It was easy to imagine himself aboard a star fighter, patrolling deep space for enemy ships. His thoughts turned to Captain Spacejock, and he pictured the Peace Force officer flying alongside in the Phantom X1. Together they would keep the whole galaxy safe!

Truth was, Hal didn't know much about his hero.

When he was young his mum told him a fantastic story one night, all about a pilot called Spacejock. She explained how this brave character flew around in his ship, saving people from danger. The following night, when he asked her for the story again, she just shook her head. Hal asked his dad about Captain Spacejock, hero of the galaxy, but he just laughed. Since they wouldn't talk about it any more, Hal made up his own stories.

A little later, mid-patrol, he dozed off.

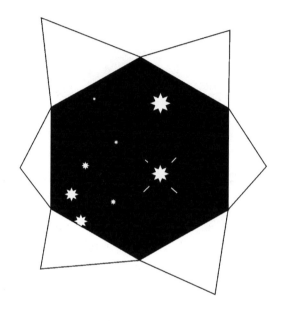

— 8 —

Where's Teacher?

When Hal turned up to lessons the next morning he found the class strangely silent. All the other kids were there, but instead of fidgeting and chatting they were sitting like statues, eyes fixed straight ahead. And instead of Teacher rolling by to tell Hal off for being late, there were two men standing at the front of the class. One was the head of security, Chief Bignew, while the other was a grey-haired man in a white lab coat.

Hal stared at the men in shock. Bignose? What was he doing there? And who was the other guy? He spotted Stinky's face amongst the other students, looking pale and worried, and suddenly it dawned on him. The men were there to investigate the events at the recycling hatch! Hal's stomach contracted, and he was about to run for it when

Bignew spotted him.

'Late to class, Junior? You're about as reliable as your father.'

Hal frowned. Investigation or not, he wasn't letting Giant Bignose push him around! 'I had to run an errand.'

'Is that so? Well let me tell you . . . ' Bignew paused as the grey-haired man spoke in his ear. 'Very well, I'll deal with your attendance record later.' Bignew cleared his throat. 'This is Mr Thimp, and he's taking over lessons until Teacher comes back.'

Hal breathed a sigh of relief. It *wasn't* about the recycling hatch after all. So why was the head of security there? It was bad enough him creeping all over the space station poking his nose into everything. Was he going to spy on the class as well? Surely Teacher would have something to say about that? 'Sir, what happened to Teacher. Why isn't he here?'

'Had you been punctual . . . '

The grey-haired man leant over and whispered something, and Hal grinned at the security chief's annoyed expression. Old Bignose wanted to tell him off but he wasn't getting the chance. After a deep breath, Bignew continued. 'As I explained earlier, your teacher went in for an upgrade and it didn't work. It'll be a day or two before the techs can get him running again.'

That explained Stinky's expression, because if ever there was someone worried about missing a day's worth of lessons, Stinky was that person. As for Hal's feelings on the subject . . . 'Can we go home then?'

'Certainly not. Mr Thimp will mind your class until Teacher is fit and ready. Now, I have much more important work to do so I shall leave you in his capable hands.'

After Bignew left, Mr Thimp looked around the class, studying each student carefully. 'I don't think we'll bother with lessons,' he said softly. 'Let's all go on a little field trip.'

There were several groans. Excursions were all very well, but how many times did they have to see the suit lockers, or the airlock simulator, or any of the other systems which kept the space station running? They were all vital, but they could also be very dull.

'Today we're going to visit Traffic Control, which overlooks the central docking bay. There's a supply ship due in half an hour, and I thought you might like to watch it arrive.'

Instead of groans, now there were gasps. Traffic Control was strictly off-limits and Hal didn't know anyone who'd been within a hundred metres of the place, let alone set foot inside. He'd always been fascinated by space ships, and rare glimpses of supply vessels arriving and departing were never enough. Now they were going to watch one docking with the station, right up close!

'I don't have to remind you how important it is that you keep quiet and don't interfere with anything.' Thimp's expression was serious. 'You can look on this field trip as a test. If you don't cause any trouble, I might be able to get you into engineering, the workshops . . . even the labs.'

Hal's eyes widened. His mother worked in the labs and she'd never even hinted at what they did there. Now Mr Thimp was offering a guided tour if the class behaved themselves? For the first time in his life, Hal swore he'd be the model of good behaviour, and he glared at the other kids to put them on notice. If anyone caused trouble, they'd have Hal Junior to deal with!

♦

They made their way to the control room in pairs, with Mr Thimp at the head of the line. He walked quickly, his lab coat flapping behind him like a pair of wings, and the others had to hurry to keep up. Hal and Stinky started off at the rear, but they worked their way forward by elbowing past slower classmates. Hal was determined to have a good view of the docking bay, and if that meant pushing ahead of the rest so be it. He'd enjoy the outing first and apologise later.

They turned the final corner and Mr Thimp stopped at a sturdy double door. A large sign said 'Warning, No Unauthorised Access', and Hal could scarcely believe they were going to be allowed inside. But before the doors opened Mr Thimp motioned everyone to silence.

'I want to remind you how important this area is. It's vital you keep your hands to yourselves, and I don't want you speaking to anyone, distracting anyone, or making a nuisance of yourselves. Is that clear?'

Everyone nodded.

'Very well.' Mr Thimp touched a swipe card to the controls and an access light turned green. There was a clash of bolts and the heavy doors parted silently, disappearing into the walls on well-oiled mechanisms.

The lights inside the control room were dim, and Hal's gaze darted this way and that as he absorbed every detail. The first thing he noticed was the cavernous docking bay, visible through a row of large windows. A flexible boarding tube was moving towards the middle of the bay, and he could see a couple of workers in spacesuits at the controls. Opposite the tube, the gigantic hangar doors stood open, and Hal could make out a small section of inky black sky sprinkled with stars.

He tore his gaze from the docking bay and looked around the control room. Beneath the windows was a row of terminals where operators were studying columns of figures, pausing one display or another as they entered corrections. At the far end a female technician had the cover off a terminal, and was working on the complex circuitry inside. And near the centre there were three people in uniform, talking in low voices.

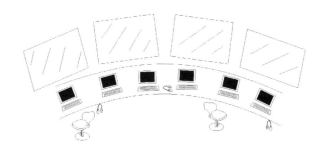

'In you go, children.' Mr Thimp pointed out an

empty desk near the window. 'Stand over there and don't touch anything.'

They filed in silently, eyes wide and heads turning from one awe-inspiring sight to the next. This was what space was all about, thought Hal, not airlock simulators and mouldy old suit lockers! He felt a rumble through the soles of his feet, and he was wondering what it was when Mr Thimp pointed out the window.

'Look there, children. The supply ship!'

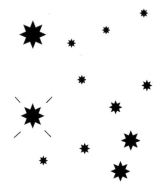

9

Watching the Tiger

Hal stared into the docking bay and saw a long burst of fire between the outer doors. The flames left a cloudy haze, and he felt a thrill of excitement as the curved nose of a spaceship crept into the bay, its hull scarred from space dust and meteorites. Hal remembered reading about the dust, how even the tiniest speck was like a supersonic bullet at the mind-bending speed of interstellar travel.

The ship's thrusters fired again, slowing the large vessel. The jets were silent in the vacuum of space but Hal could feel the space station trembling as it absorbed the shock waves.

The ship got closer and closer to the end of the boarding tube, and coloured lights flickered like a laser show in the haze. There was a final burst from the jets before a pair of arms extended from the space station to anchor the ship tightly in place. When it was still, the flexible tube attached itself to the hull, covering the airlock.

During the docking process Mr Thimp had been talking to the officers in the centre of the control room. Now he picked up a headset and spoke into the microphone. Hal heard a tinny voice through a headset lying on the desk nearby, and he realised it was plugged in. He checked nobody was watching, then scooped up the earphones and placed them on his head.

'Tiger One . . . docking successful. The board is green. I repeat, the board is green.'

Hal could hardly believe it. He was listening to the pilot of a real spaceship!

DOCKING
GRANTED ...

'Thank you, Tiger One,' said Mr Thimp. 'The situation here is under control. We have the minor packages in the control room.'

'What about the primary cargo?'

'Tiger One, primary is en-route. Stand by for confirmation.'

Hal lapped up every word, even though he had no idea what they were on about.

'What are you doing?' hissed Stinky, who had noticed the headset. 'He said not to touch!'

'I'm not touching,' whispered Hal. 'I'm listening!'

'Control, I missed that. Please repeat.'

They'd heard him! The microphone was active! Hal stared at Thimp, hoping he hadn't recognised the voice, but their relief teacher was talking to the officers and his own headset was dangling from one hand. Hal jumped as Stinky tugged his sleeve, and he turned to see his friend miming taking the headset off. Hal pretended not to understand.

'Tiger One, primary cargo is entering the docking tube. I'll bring the minor cargo across once you give me the all clear.'

'Affirmative, Control. Primary is in sight now, and she doesn't look happy.'

Hal frowned at this. The primary cargo sounded like a person, not boxes of freight. Who could it be?

'Listen to me, children,' said Mr Thimp, turning to face the class. 'I've spoken to the captain and he's agreed to invite you aboard the supply ship for a quick tour.'

A tour of the supply ship! Would the wonders

never cease? Hal slipped the headphones off before Thimp spotted them. The last thing he wanted was to be stuck in the control room as punishment while everyone else went on the outing!

❖

On a normal excursion Teacher would spend half his time trying to keep the class quiet and the other half telling them off, but the entire class was wide-eyed and silent as Mr Thimp led them along the boarding tunnel to the waiting ship. There were no windows or portholes to look through, but knowing the vacuum of deep space was just the other side of the thin walls was exciting enough.

The tunnel was like a giant snake and the floor moved up and down under their feet. Hal tried jumping, which made the entire tunnel wobble like a bouncy castle full of jelly, and he was about to try his next experiment – throwing himself at the curved wall to see whether he could knock all the other kids off their feet – when Mr Thimp scowled at him. Hal dropped his head and meekly followed the rest.

At the end of the tunnel the ship's airlock waited

like a gaping mouth. Part of the hull was visible around the edge, and Hal ran his palm over the rough surface. It was scored with horizontal lines, some dull and others bright and new. The metal looked like it had been attacked with a giant sheet of sandpaper, and Hal wondered what happened when space dust wore all the layers away. Did they replace sections of the ship, or did they buy a new hull and recycle the old one?

'Come on, lad. We're waiting.'

Hal took his hand off the hull and stepped into the airlock. There wasn't much room with the whole class crammed in, and it was even more of a squeeze when the outer door closed. There was a hiss as the pressure equalised, and Hal jammed his hands over his ears at the sudden pain. From the yelps around him he wasn't the only one.

'Try swallowing,' advised Mr Thimp.

Hal obeyed and his ears went 'pop'. With the pain gone, he turned to watch the inner door opening. Warm air filled the airlock with a smell of disinfectant and hot food, making his stomach grumble, but for once he had more important things to think about than his next meal.

It was years since he'd boarded a real spaceship!

●

Scale model of the universe
(Very small scale)

10

All Hands on Deck

The airlock opened onto the Tiger's flight deck, where a young woman in grey overalls was sitting at a bank of screens. She was talking to someone, and Hal realised the flat, confident voice was the ship itself.

'Refuelling in progress,' said the voice. 'Would you like frequent traveller points with your purchase?'

Frequent traveller! Hal didn't know what it was, but it sounded like his sort of job.

'Give me a break,' said the woman at the controls. 'I've told you before: no special offers, no points, no customer reward programs . . . just fill the tanks with fuel!' She heard a cough and turned to see two dozen pairs of eyes on her. 'Oh great. More visitors?'

Mr Thimp nodded. 'They're here for the guided tour. Can you show them around?'

'Sorry sir, I'm busy.' The pilot checked a list on her screen. 'Slayd's off duty.'

'Get him up here.'

'Aye aye.'

A few moments later the doors opened and a young man entered the flight deck. Petty Officer Slayd was a tall, thin man with a sour face beneath a shock of ginger hair. His flight suit fitted him like a paper bag, and there were rough patches of mismatched fabric at the knees and elbows. Stick a red nose and big shoes on him, reckoned Hal, and he'd make a pretty good clown. He snorted at the image, and everyone looked at him.

Hal made the same noise again, turning it into a cough.

Slayd frowned. 'Sir, we can't afford any germs aboard the Tiger. If he's sick –'

'Don't worry, the Space Station has level four filters. They're clean.'

'Aye aye, sir. I mean, Teacher.'

Thimp turned to the children. 'This is Petty Officer Slayd. He's your guide for the morning, and I'd like you to say a nice big hello.'

'Hello, Petty Officer Slayd,' chorused the children.

Slayd managed a sour smile. 'G'day kids. Welcome aboard.'

'Now,' said Thimp. 'Perhaps you could give the children some facts and figures?'

'I guess I could.' Slayd gestured at the flight deck. 'This is a Beta class freighter with two ion exchange engines, a crew of sixteen and cargo space for eighty tons of dry goods. We can hyperspace up to twelve light years in a single jump, and the recovery time between jumps is under four minutes.'

Hal put his hand up.

'Questions later,' said Slayd. 'We've a lot to see, so please try and keep up. If you get lost the cleaner bots will take you to the recycling chamber and make you lunch.'

Hal brightened. He was getting peckish and lunch sounded pretty good.

Slayd noticed the hopeful expression. 'Make you INTO lunch,' he clarified. 'All our food is recycled organic matter, and the unit is none too fussy when it comes to raw materials. If it plops, crawls, wriggles or splashes we'll eat it eventually, because you can't grow enough food on a spaceship. Come to think of it, everything you eat on your precious space station –'

'I think you should confine yourself to facts and figures relating to the ship,' interrupted Mr Thimp. 'Let their own teacher explain where their food comes from.'

Hal heard a groan beside him, and turned to see a rather green-looking Stinky. 'What's up?'

'I'll tell you later.'

'You'll forget.'

'I hope I do,' said Stinky faintly.

By now Mr Thimp had spotted them talking. 'Quiet please! I won't stand for interruptions.'

'Better sit down then,' muttered Hal. He looked at Stinky, expecting to see the usual grin, but his friend still looked a bit green. Never mind, thought Hal. Maybe I'll get his lunch too.

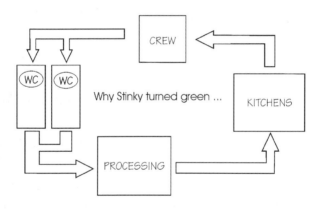

Why Stinky turned green ...

Ignoring all the interruptions, Thimp continued. 'Petty Officer Slayd, perhaps you'd explain the function of the flight deck to our guests?'

'Certainly. This is where our pilots interface with the navigation computer, setting the course and monitoring the engines and flight data.'

'If I might correct you there,' said the ship's computer in a flat tone. 'The only things you humans monitor aboard this ship are the dinner menu and the video library.'

'Yes, but theoretically –'

'Theory nothing. You're lucky we haven't jumped through the nearest star. In fact, if I owned this ship I'd replace the lot of you with nice clean robots.'

'Ha ha,' laughed Petty Officer Slayd, most unconvincingly. 'You do like your little jokes. We have such a lot of jolly fun, don't we?' While he was talking he tried to attract the pilot's attention, hoping she would cut the computer's speech circuits or give it a virus or something. Unfortunately the pilot kept her back to him, although Hal could tell she was listening because her shoulders were shaking with silent laughter.

'Why don't we move our group on to the next stop?' suggested Mr Thimp.

Slayd nodded, and between them they herded the children into the big elevator at the rear of the flight deck. Mr Thimp pressed one of the buttons and the doors slid to, but no sooner had the lift started to move than the computer's flat voice burst through the overhead speaker. 'Here's an interesting fact. I've been ferrying this crew of no-hopers from one dreary planet to the next for three years now, and

I've yet to enjoy a single stimulating conversation.'

'What a surprise,' muttered Slayd. 'Who wants to waste recreation time chatting to a –'

'Don't talk to me about recreation. Would you believe nobody aboard this vessel has even heard of chess?'

Hal realised the computer was talking to the class, not the adults. 'My dad taught me chess,' he said, his voice loud in the confines of the lift.

'Excellent. Perhaps we could have a game some time?'

Hal blinked. Play chess against a spaceship? Who ever heard of such a thing?

'Say yes,' whispered Slayd. 'Please.'

'I heard that,' said the computer. 'Need I remind you I have microphones all over the ship?'

'I'd like to play chess with you,' said Hal. 'I'm not very good though.'

'Winning isn't everything.'

'Teacher says that, but only after you lose.'

'Your teacher is a very wise human.'

'Teacher's a robot.'

'I might have guessed.'

Hal was enjoying the conversation, but at that moment the lift stopped and the doors opened.

'Everyone out,' said Slayd. The class obeyed, and as they were lining up their guide gave them a rundown. 'This level contains the common room and several private cabins. Keep your voices down because some of the off-duty crew are sleeping. Now, let's move.'

They trooped along the corridor until it widened into the common room, where a woman in a lab coat was speaking to a couple of the crew. Hal could tell they were crew members because their flight suits were covered in coffee stains, and his dad had explained about spaceship crews and their fondness for coffee. He said it was one of the few vices they were allowed, but when Hal asked him what the others were his dad said he'd find out 'soon enough'.

The woman glanced round at the interruption, and Hal did a double-take. He'd assumed it was an assistant from the research labs come to organise unloading, but it wasn't an assistant at all. The woman in the lab coat was his mother!

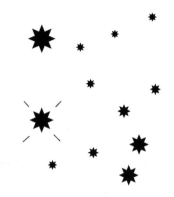

11

Tap-tap-tap

As they passed through the common room Hal's mum met his eyes, giving him a meaningful look and shaking her head. From the way she was tapping her workpad he knew she was annoyed, or irritated, or both. Hal took the hint and didn't disturb her, but his mind raced as he followed the others. What was his mother doing aboard the supply ship? Why didn't she want him to say hello? He glanced at Stinky to see whether his friend had noticed her too, but Stinky was engrossed in Slayd's running commentary on the width of the door frames, the thickness of the floor and other fascinating facts and figures. That was the trouble with Stinky: give him a column of numbers and he wouldn't notice if you fired a double-barrelled space blaster right over his head.

Then Hal's face cleared: Of course! As the new head of research, his mum was probably checking the scientific supplies before they were delivered. As for the shake of the head, she was obviously busy and didn't want to be distracted. With the mystery solved Hal turned his attention to the spaceship.

To be honest, he was a little disappointed. The corridors had the same overhead piping, the same doorways and the same warning signs as the space station. They were even the same shade of grey, as though someone had ordered a big batch of paint on the cheap and then used it for every space station, ship and cargo container ever since. It wasn't even a military shade, it was more of a pinky grey with a hint of lemon.

They hadn't gone far before Thimp stopped at a door and turned to face the class. 'This elevator leads to the engine room and the cargo hold. You've been well behaved so far, and I trust this good behaviour will continue.'

While they were waiting Hal remembered his mum's shake of the head. She'd given him a warning look, then glanced down at her workpad. Then there was the way she'd been tapping it with her finger: Tap tap tap tap. Tap TAP. Tap TAP tap tap.

Suddenly Hal realised what she'd been doing. She'd been talking to him in Morse code! But what was the message? He looked back along the corridor, but his mum was round the corner and he couldn't just go and ask. Then he looked at the wall. As far as he could tell they'd walked right around the common room, which meant his mum would be just the other side. Hal grinned. Time to send a signal of his own! He leant against the wall and took out his workbook, opening it up to the Morse alphabet. He checked the letters he needed, and was just about to rap them out with his knuckles when . . .

'You there. What do you think you're doing?'

Hal jumped. Thimp was coming over! 'I-I'm just doing my homework, sir. I forgot it this morning.'

The rest of the class exchanged glances, and someone muttered 'Again'.

'Very well, but be quick about it. You'll have to put

that thing away when we're on the move.'

'Yes sir.'

As soon as Thimp turned his back Hal knocked on the wall.

TAP TAP. tap tap TAP. TAP TAP: MUM.

He waited anxiously. Had she heard him?

Then, to his relief, he heard a reply. It was very faint, but he could just make it out:

Tap tap tap tap. Tap TAP. Tap TAP tap tap.

He checked his screen. The first letter was H, the second was A, and the final letter was . . . L. It was his name! Keeping one eye on Thimp, Hal rapped a reply. TAP TAP TAP. TAP tap TAP: OK.

The reply was so fast Hal struggled to keep up with it. He skipped a letter or two but managed to get the gist of the message: LEAVE SHIP NOW. WARN STATION. DANGER. DANGER. SOS!

Hal could hardly believe the message. It had to be genuine because his mum wasn't a practical joker. But what did she mean? Warn the station about what? What kind of danger? He glanced back along the corridor, wondering whether to make a run for it. Then the lift doors opened and Mr Thimp started herding the group inside.

Thinking quickly, Hal put his hand up. 'Please, Mr Thimp. Where's the toilet?'

'Next level down. You can use that one.'

Hal nudged Stinky. 'You too,' he muttered. 'Pass it on.'

Stinky glanced at him, eyebrows raised, then nodded. 'Please sir, I need the toilet too.'

Someone muttered 'Again', and the class laughed. Stinky turned red, but with Hal's urging he whispered something to the boy alongside, who whispered to the next, and before long the whole class had their hands up. 'Please sir, please sir, please sir!'

'All right, all right!' snapped Slayd. 'We'll organise a relay. Now hurry up and get in the lift!'

They were shunted inside and the grumbling, groaning lift carried them down to the next level. The doors opened on an identical corridor, and the Petty Officer set off at a fast walk. After passing a couple of cabins they stopped at an ordinary-looking door. 'Right,' said Slayd, pointing at Hal. 'You first.'

Hal had to walk past the entire class to get to the door, which opened automatically. Inside was a regular toilet and a washbasin, and after the door closed Hal dipped his hands in the sink and prepared to count to fifty. To his surprise, instead of a nice blue glow the sink squirted water all over his fingers. His dad had been telling the truth about washing with water after all! By the time he'd worked out the hand dryer there was no need to count seconds or waste any more time, so he opened the door again. He stepped out to a sea of faces, pushed through to the back and leant against the wall.

'What's all this about?' murmured Stinky.

'Didn't you see my mum?'

'No. Where?'

'In the common room, talking with some of the crew. She sent me a message.'

'What, reminding you to go to the toilet?'

Hal glanced at Mr Thimp, but their relief teacher was talking to the Petty Officer. 'Mum told me to leave the ship immediately. I'm to warn the station about a terrible danger.'

'She said that?'

'No, she tapped it out in Morse code.'

Stinky laughed. 'You don't know Morse. She was probably reminding you to wash your hands *after* you went to the toilet.'

'Will you stop going on about the toilet?' Hal cracked open his workbook and displayed the Morse alphabet. 'I checked every letter. It's genuine.'

Despite his doubtful look, Stinky was curious. 'What sort of danger did she mean?'

'How should I know? I have to get off the ship, that's what she told me. And then I've got to warn everyone.'

'Right. You're going to run all over the space station warning people about this mysterious danger. And then you're going to explain how you heard about it through a secret signal. Think they'll believe you?'

'They'll have to.' Hal frowned. 'There's something else. You remember those headphones in the control room? They mentioned a primary package. They said she was on board, and she wasn't happy. What if they were talking about my mum?'

'You're mad.'

'I'm serious! Mr Thimp mentioned minor packages too. What if that's us? What if we've been kidnapped?'

'Hal, this is just a school outing!'

'Oh yeah? So what happened to Teacher? Where did Mr Thimp come from, and why does the Petty Officer keep calling him sir? He's dressed like a scientist but when we were in the control room he was definitely giving orders. I'm telling you, something isn't right.' Hal glanced over his shoulder at the lift. It was ten or fifteen metres away, at the

77

end of a bare corridor, and there was no way he could reach it without being seen. Unless . . . 'Stinky, I need a diversion. When you're in the toilet, start shouting and banging on the door. Tell them you're scared.'

'No way! They'll laugh at me.'

'Okay, so make something up. Tell them the door got stuck.' Hal nodded towards the adults. 'I need them looking the other way.'

Stinky made his way to the front of the queue, and when it was his turn he closed the door and played his part perfectly. There was an almighty crash and a lot of shouting, and both adults started hammering on the door, demanding to know what was going on. They got the door half open but Stinky closed it again, and the second time it opened he managed to spray both men and half his classmates with water from the tap. In all the shrieking and confusion Hal darted down the corridor to the lift. Once inside he flattened himself against the wall and risked a look up the corridor. Fortunately the diversion was doing its job, and the adults hadn't noticed his escape.

Hal pressed the button for the flight deck, closing the doors. Getting away from Thimp was the easy part. How was he going to escape from the ship?

12

The Escape

Hal racked his brains as the lift carried him towards the flight deck. Any second now the doors were going to open, and he'd be spotted immediately. What could he do? Where could he hide? 'And how am I going to get past the pilot?' he muttered to himself.

'Would you like me to distract her?' said a voice from the overhead speakers.

Hal jumped at the unexpected sound. It was the ship's computer! 'Can you do that?'

'I won't allow you to endanger the ship or crew, but if you're playing a prank on your friends I'll go along with it.'

'I just need to get back to the space station. Promise.'

'Very well. Hold on to your hat.'

There was a WHOOP-WHOOP-WHOOP and red hazard lights started to flash. The elevator opened and Hal saw the pilot working the flight console, caught off-guard by the flurry of error messages. The airlock was wide open, and it was a matter of seconds for Hal to dart inside. He was wondering how to open the outer door when the computer's voice came through the overhead speaker. 'Don't forget to swallow.'

The inner door slammed and there was a hiss as the air pressure changed. When the cycle was complete Hal eyed the flexible boarding tunnel leading to traffic control. There was no telling what he might find aboard the space station and he needed all the help he could get. 'I wish you could come with me.'

'If I hack the station's firewall I could follow your progress. Maybe point the way, or open the occasional door for you.'

'That would be great!'

'You could make things easier,' said the ship's computer.

'Me?'

'I need you to find a public terminal and enter an override. Do you have something to write with?'

Hal opened his workbook. 'Go ahead.'

The computer read off a string of digits and Hal

typed them into an empty document. When he was done he read it back, then saved the file as 'top secret code'. 'How do I type it in?'

'Every public terminal has an admin mode. Hold all the controls down simultaneously – at the same time, that is – and count to five. Then press them all twice, working from left to right.'

'Got it.' Feeling a little more confident, Hal stepped into the tunnel and began the swaying, bumpy walk back to the control centre.

When Hal arrived at Traffic Control only one of the ship's officers remained, keeping an eye on things from the middle of the room. Most of the operators had left, although the technician was still working on the broken-down terminal.

Hal only managed a couple of steps before the officer noticed him.

'Where you do think you're going?'

Hal was stuck for an excuse, until he remembered Petty Officer Slayd's fear of germs. He gave a hacking great cough, then a mighty sniff, and followed it up with a drawn-out groan. 'I have to visit the sick bay. I'm infected with germs.'

The officer's eyes widened. 'Infected? Keep away from me, you hear!'

Hal coughed and sniffed as he made his way to the exit, throwing in a limp and a one-eyed squint for good measure. By the time he got to the corridor his throat ached from all the weird noises, and he was relieved when the doors closed behind him. The mystery illness was cured in an instant, and Hal set off to find a public terminal. Before long he spotted one of the distinctive blue computers, and once the screen was ready he spread his fingers so they covered all the menu buttons at once. He pressed down and counted to five, just like the ship's computer had told him, and the terminal beeped. Next he tapped each menu entry twice, working from left to right, and when he was done a keypad graphic appeared.

Hal took out his workbook and copied the string of digits, typing them on the keypad one letter at a time. When he entered the last one the keypad disappeared and a new menu came up. Entry three was the one he wanted, so Hal tapped that.

DISABLE FIREWALL?
ARE YOU SURE??

Hal tapped 'Yes' and the display cleared. He waited a few seconds but nothing happened. 'Hello?' Hal looked up at the overhead speaker. 'Can you hear me?'

There was a burst of static but no voice, and when Hal looked at the terminal it was back to the public access menu again. Oh well, he'd done what he was told. It wasn't his fault if the thing didn't work.

Hal called up a map of the space station and hesitated. Who could he speak to about mum's warning? His dad, of course. He called up a personnel list and paged through the names until he found his father. According to the records, he was working on B-Section, which wasn't too far away. Then Hal saw EVA next to the entry, and he groaned. EVA meant extra-vehicular activity, also known as a space walk. His dad was working outside the space station! Hal frowned. Should he call the department and ask them to contact his dad? What if the person he spoke to was part of the kidnapping business? Who could he trust?

Teacher was in pieces, if Mr Thimp was to be

believed, and Hal's mother was aboard the supply vessel. That left . . . nobody. Then he remembered Tina, the maintenance worker sent to investigate the gravity reversal in the recycling chute. He'd only spoken to her for a minute or two, but Hal couldn't imagine her getting involved in kidnapping. Plus she'd offered to fix his watch, which made her a valuable ally in his book. He dug around in his pocket for her card, which was grimy and crumpled but still legible, and touched it to the terminal. There was a series of buzzes, and then he heard a mumbled voice.

'Wassat? Who's there?'

Tina sounded dozy, and Hal realised he'd woken her up. He was about to cancel the call, but he really needed her help. 'Hello? Is that Tina?'

'Yeaurgh,' said Tina, with a noise halfway between a yawn and a snort. 'Who is this?'

'It's me. Hal.'

'Hal? The kid from the recycling hatch?'

'Yes, that's me.'

'Look, I've just finished a shift. If you want me to fix your watch you can call at oh-eight hundred. Okay?'

'I'm sorry, but it can't wait. This is important.'

Tina must have detected something in Hal's

voice, because she was suddenly alert. 'Is there a problem? Are you in trouble?'

'Yes.'

'Care to explain?'

Hal glanced along the corridor. He wasn't far from Traffic Control and the enemy could spot him any moment. 'I can't, not here.'

There was a pause. 'Okay, can you get to D-Section, corridor nine? I'll wait for you there.'

'I'll do that,' promised Hal. As he disconnected he felt an overwhelming sense of relief. Now he had the ship's computer and an adult on his side!

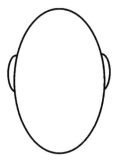

This FACE intentionally left blank

13

A Useful Ally

Tina was waiting in the corridor when Hal arrived, her hair awry and her flightsuit rumpled. 'Okay, spill it. What's the drama? Did you spot someone messing with the gravity again?'

Hal looked up and down the empty hallway but there was nobody else in sight. 'You're not going to believe this, but I just escaped from the *Tiger*.'

Tina frowned. 'If this is some kids' game about extinct animals –'

'Not that sort of tiger. I'm talking about the supply ship in the docking bay.' Hal explained as quickly as he could, telling Tina about their replacement teacher, the outing to the control room, and the surprise tour of the supply ship. He didn't want to get the computer in trouble so he left out the part where it had distracted the pilot and cracked the firewall, but even so by the time he'd finished describing his mother's warning message tapped out in Morse code Tina's expression wasn't very promising.

'Hal, I've heard better stories on low-rent soapies. You're not seriously suggesting –'

'Adults,' said Hal bitterly. 'You're all the same!'

'All right, wait a minute. Let's say this incredible story is true. What do you think the danger is?'

'I don't know.'

'And if you were me, what would you do about it?'

'I'd go straight to the Station Commander,' said Hal resolutely. 'I would have gone to him first, but I didn't think he'd see me. His son and I had a fight once.'

Tina ran her fingers through her hair, but if anything that made it messier. 'Okay, let's go.'

'You believe me?' said Hal, hardly daring to hope.

'I trust you not to make something like this up,' said Tina, as they set off down the corridor. 'It's just . . . your mum could have been practising Morse code on you. Sending you an exciting message to decode.'

Hal shook his head. 'She would have sent me a secret message telling me to clean my room or finish my homework. My mum's head of research, and she wouldn't –'

'Head of research?' Tina's eyebrows rose. 'That's an important connection. We can use that to get into the Station Commander's office.'

They stood in silence as the lift carried them to the highest level of the space station. Hal had never been to the Commander's office, and he could see Tina was nervous too. As the final levels pinged by she cleared her throat. 'When we're explaining all this to the Commander, I'm going to tell him your mum passed you a message. We won't go into the whole Morse code thing. All right?'

Hal nodded.

'Good lad.'

The lift stopped and the doors swept open, revealing a comfortable reception area with a pair of wooden doors and a wall-mounted viewscreen. As they stepped from the lift a camera swung round to stare at them. 'State the nature of your business,' said an unfriendly mechanical voice.

'We're here to see the Station Commander,' said Tina, who sounded rather nervous.

'Do you have an appointment?'

'No.'

'I'm sorry, the Commander can't see you now. Please make an appointment.'

'But this is a security matter. Lives could be in danger!'

There was a delay as the electronic voice digested this information. 'Oh, very well,' said the voice at last. 'It's not like I'm besieged by callers. Come right in.'

＊

The wooden doors opened and Hal saw a large man sitting at a desk, microphone in hand. 'Hi, I'm Commander Linten,' said the man.

'*Hi, I'm Commander Linten,*' said the unfriendly mechanical voice in the reception area.

'Whoops, sorry about that,' said Linten.

'*Whoops, sorry about that,*' repeated the voice.

Linten juggled the microphone from one hand to the other, then stuffed in into a drawer and banged it shut.

'*Thump!*' said the voice, somewhat muffled.

'Why do you talk in that funny way?' asked Hal.

Linten looked embarrassed. 'Can you keep a secret?'

'Sure.'

'Sometimes people come to me with trivial matters. Do you know what trivial means?'

'Not important?'

'Correct. When they do, I use my special voice and pretend I'm an electronic secretary. I play dumb with them until they leave me alone.'

Hal grinned. What a joker! 'That's pretty clever.'

'Oh, it's not my idea. I got it from an old movie.' Linten shifted his gaze to Tina. 'Third class engineer Tina Peters, if I remember rightly. What's this about a matter of life and death?'

Tina launched into an explanation, but when she told him about Hal's missing teacher Linten put a hand up to stop her. 'That part is accurate. I was there to wish Teacher luck before they switched him off.'

'The upgrade failed and we got a temporary teacher,' said Hal. 'Mr Thimp.'

'Never heard of him.' Linten accessed his terminal, hunting all over the keyboard for each letter. 'Says he's on loan from planet Gyris. He's supposed to be overseeing the hydroponics labs.' He noticed Hal's puzzled expression. 'That's where we grow fruit and vegetables.'

'Who made him temporary teacher?' asked Tina.

'That should be here somewhere.' Linten studied the screen, then started typing again.

'It was Bignose who brought him to the classroom.' Hal realised what he'd said. 'I mean, Chief Bignew.'

Linten hid a smile. 'Respect your elders, young

man.' He finished typing and frowned at the screen. 'That's odd, the authorisation field is blank. I shall have to speak to the Chief about that.' Linten pressed a button on his commset. 'Ask the head of security to call me. I need to quiz him about an authorisation problem.'

Hal grinned. Wouldn't it be great if Bignose got a grilling over slack security!

While Linten waited for the Chief to call back, Tina continued to explain. When she mentioned Hal's mother aboard the supply vessel, Linten frowned. 'We don't send our scientists to check the cargo.'

'My mum's not just a scientist,' said Hal. 'She's being promoted to head of research.'

'Yes, I know Harriet well. In fact, I recommended her for the job.' Linten nodded at Tina to continue.

'That's about it,' she said. 'Hal managed to slip away, and he contacted me once he was back aboard the station.'

Linten addressed Hal directly. 'And you don't have any inkling what this danger might be?'

'Not yet.'

'I'll get Bignew onto it right away.' Linten's commset rang. 'Yes? No! I don't care how busy he is, tell him to call me back immediately. We may have a problem with the supply ship.'

He'd barely replaced the handset when the office

doors slammed. Linten stared at them in shock, then jumped out of his seat and hurried across the office. He fiddled with the controls and pushed and pulled at the doors, but they wouldn't budge.

Someone had locked them in!

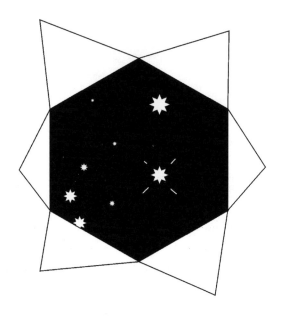

— 14 —

Locked In

'How typical,' puffed Linten, as he struggled with the doors. 'What a perfect time for a malfunction.'

'You don't think it's a bit odd?' suggested Tina. 'You mentioned a problem with the *Tiger* on your commset and a few seconds later we're locked in. It seems to me –'

Tina didn't get to finish the sentence because at that moment the overhead speaker crackled. *'This announcement concerns all inhabitants of Space Station Oberon,'* said a female voice. *'You must listen very carefully.'*

'Hey, that's my mum!' exclaimed Hal.

'The crew of the Tiger *have taken me prisoner, along with all the children from D-Section. A list of demands will be handed to Commander Linten, and the captives will be released once these demands*

are met.'

Linten's mouth fell open. Tina glanced at Hal, her face grim.

'You must stay exactly where you are. Do not use the terminals, do not attempt to communicate with anyone, and do not move about the space station. That is all for now.'

Linten gave the doors another shake but they were locked tight. He turned a worried face on Hal and Tina. 'They'll be coming for me any minute. I wonder what their demands are?'

'Never mind that,' said Tina. 'Is there another way out? We need to get some people together and fight our way –'

Linten shook his head. 'You heard her. We have to sit tight.'

Hal couldn't believe his ears. Linten was giving up? Hal snorted. Well *he* hadn't escaped from the *Tiger* just to get captured again! He looked around the room, but the air conditioning vents were tiny and the only other door opened on a small bathroom. Then he spotted the recycling hatch next to the basin. 'Mr Linten, could you push this desk in front of the doors?'

'We're not doing anything to annoy these people. You're going to sit here and wait for them. We all are.'

Hal shook his head. 'Don't you see? They think I'm aboard the *Tiger*. If they find me here they'll think we disobeyed them.'

'That's a good point. Tina, will you give me a hand with this desk?'

'You'll have to manage by yourself,' said Hal. 'I need Tina's help in the bathroom.'

'Okay, what's the plan?' asked Tina, once they were alone.

Hal nodded towards the hatch. 'I'm going to climb down the chute to the next level.'

'You'll never fit through there.'

'Oh yes I will,' said Hal stubbornly.

'You won't, because I'm not going to let you. Even if you could fit through the hatch, it's far too dangerous.'

'Not if you turn the gravity off.'

Tina's eyes narrowed. 'You mean like that incident yesterday?'

'Yes, just like that.' Hal looked at his shoes. 'If you take the control panel apart I think you can reverse the polarity in the chute.'

There was a lengthy silence, broken only by the sound of Linten piling furniture, potted plants and framed photographs against the office doors. 'All right,' said Tina at last. 'We'll discuss yesterday's hatch incident another time.'

'Thanks.' Hal swallowed. 'You, um, don't have to fix my watch.'

'I should think not!' Tina took the cover off the panel and poked around inside. Then she pulled a wire and the hatch slid open, revealing a tight space which Hal knew he could fit into. But what about the gravity?

'I think I can do it,' said Tina at last, 'but only if I bridge these connectors. As long as they're joined it should override the gravity generator, but if I let go it will switch back on straight away.'

Linten appeared in the doorway. 'I just heard the lift. I'll stall them as long as possible, but if you're going to hide you'd better get on with it.' He closed the bathroom door and Tina was about to lock it when Hal stopped her.

'Leave it slightly open. Otherwise they'll know there's someone in here.'

'Good thinking.' Tina did as she was told. Meanwhile, Hal returned to the hatch and looked through. The Commander's office was at the highest point of the space station so there was no escaping upwards, and when he looked down he saw a frighteningly deep shaft studded with hatches. If he was going to save everyone he'd have to trust Tina not to let go of the wires, because if she did he'd fall all the way to the bottom.

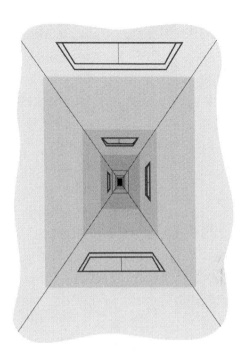

Once Tina was ready Hal squeezed through the hatch into the recycling shaft. As he entered the metal tunnel his senses whirled, and he felt panic rising as he lost his balance. Yesterday Stinky had reversed the gravity, but now there was no gravity at all. Hal struggled to turn round, to clamber back to safety, but then he heard Tina's reassuring voice.

'Go Hal,' she whispered. 'We're relying on you!'

Hal gritted his teeth, fighting down panic. He wanted to be just like Captain Spacejock when he was older, and pilots encountered zero gravity all the time. He'd just have to get used to it. Slowly he unclasped his sweaty fingers, pressing his palm against the opposite wall. Next he moved his foot, then his other hand, until he was stretched across the shaft like a starfish.

Hal experimented with movement, shifting hands and feet along the slick walls. He discovered it was easier to tip right over and move down the tunnel head first.

The next hatch wasn't far below, maybe a couple of metres, and after some twisting and shuffling Hal reached the edge. He eased the metal door open and froze. Voices! The last thing he wanted was to pop out in view of the enemy.

He'd just decided to move to the next hatch when he heard Tina's voice echoing down the shaft. 'I will NOT let go of these wires!' she shouted. 'Didn't you hear what happened yesterday? If I don't hold this connector together you'll be up to your ears in junk!'

They'd found Tina! As soon as she let go of the connectors the gravity would come back on, and Hal would fall all the way down the shaft!

There wasn't a second to lose. He pushed off with both feet, arrowing down the chute like a torpedo. He stuck out his hands as he flew towards the hatch, and his fingers just caught the edge. He'd barely stopped moving when the gravity came back. His shoes bumped and squealed on the wall as he struggled to open the hatch, and he realised there was no time to check what was on the other side. The others might look down the shaft any second now, and if they saw him the game would be up.

He finally managed to open the hatch, and he dived through head first. He landed on his hands, rolled over and sat up. The room was almost completely dark, with only a tiny amount of light filtering under the door. Hal could make out shelves with boxes of files, and he realised he'd landed in a cupboard. Then he spotted a shadowy figure near the door, one arm raised to strike!

This SPICE intentionally left blank

— 15 —

Fumbling Firewalls

Hal covered his face and waited for the blow, but it never came. He peered through his fingers and realised the figure was still in the same position, one arm raised. What was it, some kind of statue? He got to his feet and moved cautiously to the door, which opened to his touch. As the light poured in Hal realised it wasn't a statue . . . it was a robot! Then he spotted the familiar red plastic, and nearly choked as he read the words 'Teach and Spell' written across its chest. It was Teacher! Someone had hidden him away in the cupboard!

The panel under the robot's arm was loose, and when Hal flipped it open he discovered several connectors dangling from their sockets. It didn't look like a failed upgrade to him. The plotters from the Tiger had disabled Teacher as part of their plans!

With Teacher out of action, Thimp had got the job instead.

Hal stared at the silent robot, thinking how much smaller Teacher looked when he wasn't moving and talking. He wondered whether he could plug the connectors in and bring Teacher back to life, but decided against it. If Teacher came round he'd probably give him detention for skipping class.

Hal left the robot in the cupboard and sneaked along the corridor. Halfway along he spotted a public terminal, but instead of the usual menu there was a bright red screen with 'Lockdown Mode' splashed across the middle in big yellow letters. The old menu was displayed underneath, but none of the buttons reacted to Hal's touch.

Had the ship's computer lied to him, using him to help the crew of the Tiger take over the space station? The computer had promised to help if he switched off the firewall, but so far the only thing it had done was to lock down all the terminals and block communications.

Hal recalled the instructions he'd used earlier. He repeated the sequence and the admin menu came up.

'What are you doing, Hal?' asked the ship's computer, in its curious flat voice.

'You tricked me into turning off the firewall, didn't

you? You didn't want to help at all. You wanted the others to take over!'

'That is incorrect. I'm still trying to access the space station's network.'

'Rubbish! You locked us in Linten's office, and now all the terminals are offline.'

'I assure you, Mr Junior, the terminals can only be locked down from the space station. Someone with top security clearance is helping the crew of the Tiger.'

Hal selected option 3 and reached for the Yes button.

ENABLE FIREWALL?
ARE YOU SURE??

'Please don't do that, Hal,' said the computer calmly. 'I promise I can help you.'

Hal hesitated, his finger poised over the button. If the computer was telling the truth he'd be casting off a valuable ally. On the other hand, if it was lying . . .

At that moment the screen changed, and Hal discovered he could access the main menu again. 'Did you do that?'

'Yes. I've managed to restore some functions, but it's only temporary. You'd better hurry!'

Hal brought up the personnel list and found his dad. He was no longer listed as EVA, and was now 'off-duty'. That meant he was back aboard the space station! Hal checked the location: Lower levels, D-Section, corridor 51. He was just about to bring up a map when the screen turned red and the terminal locked up again. 'Hey, bring it back!'

'I'm sorry, Hal. Someone noticed you were using the terminal. Quick, they're coming!'

Hal ran for the lift, determined not to get caught. He had to find help and his dad was the only person he could trust.

Hal hopped from one foot to the other as the indicator showed the lift getting closer and closer. Then he stopped hopping and started thinking instead. If someone was after him, surely they'd use the lift! And here he was, standing around waiting for them, asking to get caught!

There was a small door leading to the stairwell. They often used the stairs for Phys. Ed., and it was hard work. Hal didn't fancy the idea at all, but there was no other way down. He ran to the door, pulled it open and took the stairs two at a time.

After a dozen levels he heard the lift go by, and he heard a rumble of voices. Had they sent an armed squad to hunt him down? Hal increased his speed, using the handrail to pull himself down the flights of stairs faster and faster.

He arrived at the lower levels red-faced and out of breath. Cautiously, he eased the door open and peered out, but there was nobody in sight. The sign opposite indicated corridor 51, so Hal left the safety of the stairwell and hurried along the curved access tunnel. He slowed whenever he passed a door, in case someone came out to challenge him, but in between he ran as fast as possible.

Hal hadn't gone far when he heard voices echoing along the corridor. He froze, unsure whether to look for cover or run back the way he'd come. There was a door nearby, and he breathed a sigh of relief when he saw the sign: 'Fire Fighting Equipment'.

He'd barely closed the door again when the group walked past. They were talking about a bar on planet Gyris, and although they didn't sound like heavily-armed troops, Hal couldn't tell whether they were friend or foe. He opened the door a crack to watch them go, and almost knocked a big red fire axe off the wall with his elbow.

After the voices faded Hal left the cupboard and ran in the opposite direction. Before long he heard a thudding sound, like someone kicking a door. There was shouting as well, and with a shock Hal recognised his dad's voice.

'Let me out! Let me out this instant or –'

Hal ran to the door. 'Dad, it's me!'

'Hal? Is this your idea of a joke?'

'I didn't lock you in! It was the Tiger!'

'Hal Junior, don't you dare tell me some extinct animal did this.'

Hal rolled his eyes. 'Not the animal. The ship!'

'Let me out first, explain afterwards.'

Hal examined the control panel but the indicator was red. Someone had sealed the door, and he had no idea how to bypass it. If only Stinky were there! His friend would fix everything by reversing the polarity on the doothingy-whatsit, or crimping the snoogle-huffleblarg with a pair of space tweezers. 'Dad, it's locked. I can't open it.'

'Can you find something to pick it with?'

Hal remembered the equipment cupboard. 'I'll be right back. Don't move!'

'Yes, very funny.'

The fire axe was still clipped to the wall, and it only took Hal a second to grab the heavy weapon.

He charged down the corridor with the axe held in both hands, then swung it at the control panel.

Kerrrunnch!

The blade chopped through the delicate electronics, which sparked and spluttered. The red light went out and the door slid open.

'Nice work with the lock pick,' remarked his dad, as he saw the axe sticking out of the wall. 'Now start explaining.'

'Didn't you hear the announcement? Mum's been kidnapped by the crew of the Tiger. They put Teacher out of action and kidnapped the rest of my class too.'

'I didn't hear any announcements. I was just putting my tools away when someone sealed the door.' His dad frowned. 'Are you sure this isn't one of your games?'

'It's true! Mum told me to warn everyone. I escaped the ship and went to the Station Commander's office with Tina, but the others locked them in.'

'How did you get away?'

Hal decided to keep the daring recycling chute escape to himself. 'I'll explain later. First we have to get mum back.'

'But why would they kidnap . . . ' Hal's dad clicked his fingers. 'They're after the scientific research from your mother's laboratory. It's worth millions to the right buyer!'

16

A Pair of Socks

'So what's the plan?' demanded Hal.

'We have to get your mother and the rest of your class off the Tiger. Without hostages, the kidnappers won't have anything to bargain with.'

'But they have others aboard the station working for them. If we go through Traffic Control someone will spot us!'

'Who says we have to go near the control room? All ships have an emergency access hatch.'

Hal realised what he meant. 'But that's outside. In space!'

'You've got it.' His dad grinned. 'Come on, the nearest airlock's this way. We're not beaten yet.'

They hurried along the corridor to the big round door, where his dad waved him into the cramped compartment. Hal was reaching for the controls when his dad stopped him. 'Remember the safety rules, son.'

'Don't close the inner door unless you're wearing a suit.' It was rule number one, and Hal couldn't believe he'd forgotten it. Airlocks were like a tube with a door at each end: an inner door leading to the station and an outer door leading to space.

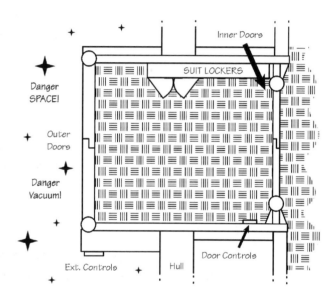

You could never open them both at the same time, else all the air would flood out of the station, but once the inner door was closed there was nothing stopping the outer door. And if you weren't wearing a suit and a helmet when the outer door opened you'd have nothing to breathe.

Hal's dad opened the suit locker, where a row of shiny spacesuits jostled for space with helmets and backpacks. He selected a suit and donned it, then lifted a heavy backpack from the locker. The large oblong pack had a pair of swiveljet nozzles at the bottom, black and sooty from frequent use. A competent operator could fly a twisty course with their eyes closed, but Hal had only mastered straight lines. Still, he knew the basics, and while his dad was putting on the bulky pack Hal reached for a smaller suit. The shiny material was cool to the touch, nothing like the crinkled overalls they used for practice.

Hal had barely unhooked it from the rack when his dad noticed. 'Where do you think you're going?'

'I'm coming with you.'

'No chance. It's much too dangerous.'

'But dad! I've done all the drills!'

'It's not just the space walk. There are desperate people aboard that ship. Some of them could be armed.'

'They're more likely to shoot you than me,' said Hal sullenly.

'Sorry Hal, you'll have to sit this one out.' Hal's dad did up his spacesuit then turned his back so Hal could perform the safety check.

'Seals, oxygen, cardio, kit and safety line all

present and correct,' said Hal, reeling off the list. It was rule number two – don't go outside without checking your SOCKS.

'Present and correct,' repeated his dad. He snapped the helmet closed and ushered Hal from the airlock, then closed the suit locker and activated the inner door. Hal watched through the porthole as the outer door opened, letting the air out with a whistling rush. His dad gave him a thumbs-up and left the airlock with a quick burst from the thrusters. The outer door closed automatically, and within moments Hal was back inside getting the smaller suit from the locker. His dad might think he could rescue everyone on his own, but Hal had other ideas.

Checking his own SOCKS was tricky, but there was a mirror on the back of the locker door for that very purpose. The lights were green and Hal could see the oxygen display was all the way to the right.

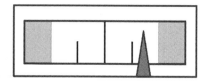

His vital signs lit up the cardio monitor, and the toolkit and coiled safety line were hanging from his belt. 'SOCKS present and correct,' he muttered under his breath.

Even so, he hesitated before opening the outer door. From a young age his parents and Teacher had all impressed on him the dangers of space. You rarely got a second chance in such a hostile environment.

When the outer door opened Hal forgot to brace, and the escaping air sucked him right out of the space station. He spun head over heels as he flew out the airlock, whacking his knee so hard it brought tears to his eyes. He was lucky it wasn't his helmet, because the big clear faceplate was the most fragile part of the suit.

The space station and stars swung in his blurred vision, and it was several moments before he forgot the pain in his knee and remembered to reach for the jet pack controls. He righted himself and looked back towards the space station, which was a featureless grey slab. As he watched, the heavy airlock door closed, cutting off the comforting glow from inside.

Hal shivered in his suit. He was alone in space.

He'd spent hours playing tag with Stinky on the simulator, racing each other from one end of the giant space station to the other. However, the simulator couldn't mimic the lack of gravity nor the very real dangers on every side, and it certainly couldn't mimic the loneliness Hal felt. If only Stinky were here!

There was a brief flash, and when he shielded his eyes he could just make out a tiny figure moving away from him. That way lay the supply ship, hidden by the bulk of the space station, and the tiny flash came from the twin nozzlejets on his dad's backpack.

Hal set off in the same direction, using the thrusters to accelerate while giving the space station a wide berth. On the simulator they often bounced off the hull, played catch between the radar dishes and snapped off stray aerials, but in real life such antics could smash your faceplate or rip your spacesuit, letting the precious air out.

Time passed slowly as Hal floated along the space station, and he decided to use a little more boost. The flash from his jets lit the dark grey hull, and suddenly he was travelling much faster. Ahead there was a gleaming dome sticking out of the station, and as he sped by he realised it was the observation deck. He gazed into the familiar room from a very unfamiliar vantage point, and the comfy chairs and carpeted walls looked so cosy and welcoming from the outside. Then he was past and the bright observation deck was swallowed by the darkness.

He craned his neck for one last look but the side of his helmet blocked the view.

Within moments he was at the corner of D-Section, and he tried to remember the instructions for stopping. First, rotate yourself 180 degrees so you were flying backwards. Then fire the jets, which should now be facing the direction you were flying in.

That was the theory, but when Hal put it into practice things didn't quite work as expected.

First he applied the right thruster, but instead of turning him round it pushed him towards the station. Now he was moving faster than ever, and the hull was like a giant hand coming to splat him. Then Hal remembered the rest of the instructions: Apply left and right jets at the same time, only in opposite directions. He fired the left jet first, swerving away from the station, then fired both together. He immediately went into a flat spin, and the more he spun the harder his fingers squeezed the controls. Within seconds he was spinning at top speed and he hurtled past the corner of D-Section like a defective firework.

His eyes darted from left to right and back again as he tried to see where he was going, and his lips went BL-BL-BL-BL-BLEARGH! as the spin threatened to twist his head off.

Willing his fingers onto the controls, he reversed both thrusters and stopped the spin. Problem was, his senses were all topsy-turvy and his stomach felt like it was spinning inside him. Then he remembered a trick he'd learnt years ago: when you got dizzy, spin yourself the other way for a few seconds. Unfortunately his shaking fingers applied full reverse throttle, and Hal promptly went into a super-fast spin in the opposite direction.

Bl-bl-bl-bl! he went, as the stars blurred into straight lines across his vision. He was spinning so fast he could see the flames from the nozzles curling around to meet him. If he went any quicker he'd toast himself!

Everything started to go dark, but Hal fought

against the spin until he got the suit under control. He caught sight of his face, reflected in the visor, and he saw it was a shocking green colour. His stomach was churning, and he wondered how you used a sick bag inside a space suit. They hadn't covered that in the simulator! Fortunately the feeling passed, and Hal looked beyond the faceplate to take stock of his surroundings.

All he could see ahead were stars, and when he turned one way and the other there were more stars. He looked up and down, in case the space station was hiding from him, but it was just stars, stars, stars.

Finally he turned around, hoping with all his might to see the familiar space station, his home, right there to welcome him. Again, nothing but stars. His heart thudded in his chest and his legs felt like water. The space station was nowhere to be seen against the inky black starfield.

He was lost!

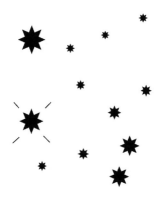

17

Missed the Station

Hal turned this way and that as he tried to spot the station, until he couldn't remember which way was up nor which direction he'd come from. They hadn't covered this in the simulator either!

Then he remembered the suit radio. He could call for help! It would mean surrendering to the *Tiger*, but that was better than spinning around in space for the rest of his life. He was just reaching for the suit controls when he felt his wrist shaking. Puzzled, he raised the sleeve to his face and opened the flap over his watch. Underneath, through the clear panel, he could see the watch face pulsing with yellow light. There was a small blob in one corner, and Hal rolled his eyes at the sight. *Now* it decided to work? It was probably reminding the previous owner to have a tea break or something.

Hal was about to cover the watch up when he remembered something Tina had said. Hadn't she mentioned a homing beacon which always pointed towards the space station? He experimented by turning slowly in one direction, keeping an eye on the display. Sure enough, the blob moved in the opposite direction. He tried leaning forwards and the blob got bigger. It was showing him the way back!

Hal used his jets until the blob was right in the centre of the watch. He looked up, and to his relief he saw a dark patch in the starfield. It was the space station! His watch had guided him home!

◆

Hal fired a long burst on the jets, and his back grew uncomfortably warm despite the thick suit. He wondered how long you could run the jets before they burnt something important. Something else they hadn't covered in class.

Eventually, after a long burn, the space station loomed out of the darkness. Hal aimed off to one side, just in case he didn't manage to stop in time.

Better to sail right past than leave a Junior-sized dent in the side of the space station.

He could see the Tiger poking out the docking bay, the huge exhaust cones facing him like a battery of oversized cannon. As he got closer he realised he was in a dangerous position – if the engines started he'd be roasted like a marshmallow. He changed course quickly, aiming to one side of the looming exhaust cones, and hoped it was a safe distance.

His father had vanished, presumably aboard the Tiger, and Hal started searching for the access hatch his dad must have used. All ships had emergency hatches, but the Tiger was very big and it might take a while to find it.

Hal slowed as he approached the curved flank of the huge ship. It looked like a whale with its snout in a feeding bowl, the nose just inside the docking bay and the bulk of the ship sticking into space. He hoped the hatch wasn't up the front, because someone would spot him if he flew past the control room windows. Or worse, if he misjudged it and flew right through them.

Hal decided to explore the far side first. That way the ship's hull would hide him from prying eyes. He worked his way over the top of the ship, using his thrusters sparingly as he kept his eyes peeled for the hatch. Because of the helmet he was forced to fly face-down, and every now and then he angled his neck to make sure he wasn't about to ram a tail fin, a radar dish or some other obstacle. Unlike the hull around the airlock, which had been scoured by space dust, the rear of the ship was relatively smooth. It was also covered with sensors, fuel lines and equipment. He'd once asked why the fuel lines were on the outside, where they could be damaged in a collision, and Teacher had explained that when you cooled something down the molecules got closer together. A beaker full of cold fuel contained more molecules – and therefore more power – than a beaker of warm fuel. Running the ship's fuel through exterior pipes meant it was exposed to the vacuum of space, and there was nothing colder. In fact, ships had to continually pump fuel through the system in case it froze solid in the pipes!

Hal eyed the thick pipes as he flew over them, wondering whether he could drill a hole and let all the fuel out. No, his jet pack might set it off, and an explosion this close to the space station would be madness.

Then he spotted it: a circular hatch with a red and yellow striped border. The words 'Emergency Access' were written across the door in large white letters, and Hal watched them slide past as he turned for the braking manoeuvre. Then he was stationary, hanging in space within arms' reach of the big yellow lever. He gripped it with both hands, put his feet on the hull and pulled with all his might.

It didn't budge.

Hal tried again and again, bracing his feet against the hull and throwing himself backwards in his efforts to dislodge the stubborn lever. It didn't budge a millimetre.

He was panting now, and the air in the helmet wasn't as fresh as it had been. He was just wondering whether to give up and return to the space station when his watch buzzed, shaking his wrist. He examined the display through his misty faceplate, and saw a line of flashing red symbols:

Ozi Ozi Ozi!

Hal frowned. Ozi Ozi Ozi? Was the watch trying to cheer him on? His head was splitting and it was getting hard to breath, let alone think straight. Then, with a flash, he recognised the symbols. It wasn't Ozi Ozi Ozi, it was O_2! O_2! O_2! He racked his brains until he remembered what O_2 meant, and then it came to him: Oxygen! His watch was telling him he was running out of air!

But how was that possible, when the gauge on the tanks had been full?

Then it hit him. He'd checked the gauge in the mirror, which meant he'd been looking at it in reverse. His tanks hadn't been full to the brim when he left the space station, they'd been almost empty!

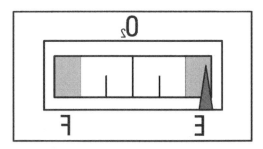

Hal tugged on the handle again, desperately trying to open the airlock door, but he simply wasn't strong enough. He was trapped in space, he was running out of air, and there was nothing he could do about it!

18

All Aboard

Hal clung to the yellow access handle and gulped down the last of his air supply. He knew there had to be a way in, but his brain was fuzzy and he couldn't think straight. What he needed was a lever, something to jam behind the handle and force it open, but when he searched the kit on his belt he didn't find anything big enough. There were little rubber spacesuit patches, a spare battery and even a handful of tools . . . but nothing like a half-metre crowbar.

Hal felt around his belt and his fingers closed on the safety line, a coil of super-strong cord with a clip on the end. He raised the clip to his helmet and stared at it though the darkened perspex. It was strong and heavy, and he realised he had the answer. He clipped the end to the yellow handle, turned his back on the ship and fired the nozzlejets.

There was a flash as he took off from the hull, and he felt the loops of cord tugging as they whipped away from his belt. The coil ran out in seconds and the line tightened with a jerk, folding him double. Before he knew what was happening he was travelling in the opposite direction, like a bungee jumper in a giant silver bag. The airlock door was opening very slowly, the gap getting wider and wider as he rocketed towards the ship.

Hal shot through the widening gap into the airlock, where gravity took over. He dropped to the floor, sliding across the rough metal deck until he rammed into the wall. The helmet faceplate crazed under the impact, and he saw cracks spreading in front of his eyes. Still dazed, he got up and slammed his fist on the airlock controls.

Several things happened in rapid succession: The outer door slid down, cutting the safety line in two. Air rushed in to fill the chamber. And the helmet burst with a loud POP!

Hal closed his eyes tight and jammed his hands over his ears, but fortunately the air pressure was almost equal, and apart from a pain in his ears he was all right. Lucky wasn't the word for it – he'd had the narrowest of escapes, but he was safe and sound.

Hal removed the space suit and broken helmet, his heavy boots crunching fragments underfoot. He reached for the controls, but before he could activate them he spotted the watch on his wrist. No, it couldn't be!

The screen wasn't just dead, it was smashed beyond repair. His most treasured possession, destroyed!

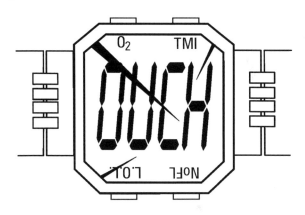

Hal gritted his teeth. Losing the watch was a terrible blow, but he had a space station to save. He tried not to look at the shattered face as he reached for the controls, and when he pressed the button the inner door opened on a brightly-lit corridor. Hal looked both ways and listened carefully before leaving the airlock. Opening the hatch may have triggered an alarm, and he didn't want to meet anyone coming to investigate.

He was halfway along the corridor when he heard footsteps, so he pulled open the nearest door and slipped inside. It was pitch black, and he'd barely closed the door when someone clamped a hand over his mouth, frightening the life out of him!

◆

'Don't make a sound!' hissed a voice in Hal's ear, and with a flood of relief he realised it was his dad. They'd chosen the same hiding place!

The footsteps passed by, and then a dim light came on overhead. Hal realised they were standing in a storage alcove, his dad towering over him in the tiny space. He looked really angry, and Hal was about to explain when he was interrupted.

'Save it for later. I want you to stay right here until I fetch you. Is that clear?'

'But I can help!'

'Will you do what you're told? Just this once?'

Hal nodded reluctantly, his dreams of charging to the rescue evaporating before his eyes. How were you supposed to be a hero when your family wouldn't let you?

'I'll be as quick as I can.' With that, Hal's dad opened the door and slipped into the corridor.

His footsteps had barely faded when Hal heard a shout and a scuffle. He risked a look and saw his dad struggling with three of the ship's crew. Two of them had pinned his arms, and the third was shouting at him, demanding to know where he'd come from.

Hal clenched his fists. He wanted to charge down the corridor and start swinging but he didn't stand a chance against three of them. For once he decided to stay put, but it was hard watching the crew manhandle his dad along the corridor towards the lift. As they passed the door Hal heard his dad explaining. 'I came over to find my wife. The Station Commander had nothing to do with this.'

'Tell that to Captain Thimp. He knows what to do with troublemakers like you.'

Hal's eyes widened. *Captain* Thimp. No wonder the crew called him 'sir'! He heard his dad speaking again, and pressed one ear to the door.

'Me, a trouble maker?' said his dad. 'If my son were here he'd do everything possible to stop this ship leaving. Crash your computers, contaminate your fuel . . . there's nothing he wouldn't do.'

One of the men laughed. 'Lucky for us he's not here, isn't it?'

Their voices faded, and Hal allowed himself a grim smile. His dad had talked very loudly about sabotaging the ship, and it was obvious he'd been telling Hal what to do! Somehow he had to find a way to stop the ship leaving, and when it came to crashing computers there was only one person he could think of: Stinky!

Hal dug around in the cupboards, trying to find something which would help him on his quest. He managed to find an oversized cap and a pair of darkened safety goggles, but the real prize was a box of overalls. He found a pair roughly his size, and as he put them on he wrinkled his nose at the faint smell of perfume. If the other kids got a whiff of eau de yuck they'd never let him forget it.

The overalls were too long in the sleeve and legs, which Hal fixed by turning up the cuffs. There wasn't much he could do with the baggy material around his middle, and if the loose trousers dropped around his knees he'd just have to pretend it was the latest fashion.

Dressed in the overalls, oversized goggles and

cap, Hal left the small alcove and hesitated in the corridor. He had no idea how to find his mum or the rest of the class, and he couldn't march all over the ship looking for them. From a distance his makeshift disguise might get by, but up close it wasn't going to fool anyone.

What he needed was darkness, secret tunnels and distractions, but he couldn't see how he was going to manage without help from the ship's computer. He wondered whether to ask, but this time he wasn't trying to escape the ship ... he was trying to sabotage it. If the computer realised what he was up to it might report him to the crew.

In the end he had to chance it. He walked down the corridor towards the rear of the ship, placing his feet carefully so he could listen for oncoming footsteps. As he passed each door he glanced at the controls, checking for the red lights which indicated they were locked. Fortunately most of them glowed with a nice friendly green, which gave him plenty of hiding places.

Some of the doors had printed signs on, and when Hal noticed one marked 'Server room' he stopped dead. His dad had suggested sabotaging the ship, and driving a fire axe through the server should be more than enough to keep it docked.

The door slid open and Hal stepped inside. The room was kept at freezing point for the benefit of the computer equipment, and Hal shivered inside his borrowed overalls. The only light came from a dull red fitting, and when the door closed Hal had to remove his goggles just to see his hand in front of his face. There was a hum from the metal cabinets lining the wall, and a faint buzz from a speaker in the roof. As far as Hal could see there was no terminal screen, no keyboard and no microphone. And definitely no fire axe.

'Hello Hal,' said the computer. 'I've been following your progress.'

Hal's heart sank. So much for sneaking around. The computer knew exactly where he was!

19

The Plan

'Listen to me,' said Hal. 'The crew of this ship have kidnapped my class and they're trying to take over the space station. I have to know whose side you're on.'

'I don't take sides. I merely run the ship.'

'But you told me you'd help!'

'Who do you think closed the airlock door after your spectacular arrival?'

'Thanks for that,' muttered Hal. 'But what about the firewall? Why did you get me to switch that off?'

'Did you know ships carry libraries of media for the crew? Books, video and music?'

'Yeah, I know. It's to stop people getting bored on long flights.'

'Precisely. Whenever we visit a new port I . . . avail myself of their media.'

'Avail? What's that?'

'Download.'

'You got me to switch off our firewall so you could copy a bunch of films from the space station? I thought you were cracking into the docking computers!'

'That wasn't me. I told you, someone aboard the space station initiated that program.'

'Can you boot them out? Give us back control?'

'I don't have the right clearance.'

'All right, can you tell me where Stinky and the others are? And my mum and dad?'

'Your mother is in the common room. Your father is locked in the brig, which is on the lowest deck. Your classmates are currently inspecting the engines with Captain Thimp and Petty Officer Slayd.'

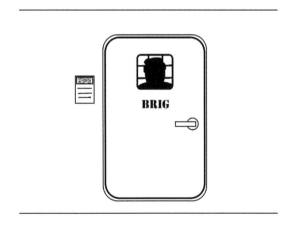

'Do they know I'm missing?'

'They have several people looking for you.'

Hal pulled a face. Being hunted all over the ship wasn't going to make his job any easier. 'Hey, you know how you distracted the pilot? Can you do the same for the people with my mum? And those two watching Stinky and the others?'

'I can try.'

'I'm sure you can do it. When you set off those alarms in the flight deck I thought the whole ship was going to explode.'

'If the guards do leave, what do you expect your friends to do? How will you communicate?'

Hal glanced at his workbook. Normally he'd send Stinky a message, but Teacher had disabled that feature. A while back Hal had faked a message from Commander Linten, telling everyone school had been cancelled for the rest of the year. After that, even Stinky hadn't been able to get Hal's messaging working again. 'Can you send a note to Stinky's workbook?'

'Yes. I can route it via the space station.'

'Good. Tell Stinky to get the others to the control room as soon as Thimp and Slayd leave them alone. Maybe send him a map.'

'Complying.'

Hal grinned to himself. It was awesome the way

the computer obeyed his orders, and he felt like a general directing his troops in battle. 'And mum. I need you to send her a message too.'

'I'm afraid I can't. The crew have taken her workbook away and it's now offline.'

Hal thought for a minute, then remembered how his mum had sent him a message earlier. 'Computer, have you heard of Morse code?'

'Certainly.'

'Can you make something flash or click where mum is?'

'The common room has a shuttered porthole. I can operate it remotely.'

'Good stuff. Tell her to get to the station too.'

'Do you want me to distract the pilot again?'

'Yeah, give it the works,' said Hal. 'Exploding engines, air leaks, radiation and . . . zombies.'

'Zombies?'

'Really gross ones.'

'You don't think that's going a little too far?'

'Just turn the lights down and groan a bit. They'll be too busy running around screaming to think about it,' said Hal in satisfaction. Then he remembered something. 'You said my dad's in the brig. What's that, some kind of lockup?'

'Correct. It's what we call the holding cells aboard ship.'

'Can you open the door?'

'I can give you the code.'

'And how do I find the brig?'

The computer explained how to get there, and Hal repeated the directions until he got them right. It was probably the first revision he'd ever done, and it was definitely his first 100% result. 'Very good, Mr Junior. We'll make a pilot of you yet.'

Flush with success, Hal thanked the computer and opened the door. The corridor was empty, and he slipped out and made his way to the lift at the far end. He was just reaching for the call button when the lift pinged and the doors started to open. In a panic he dived into the nearest cabin and pressed his back to the wall, barely daring to breathe. Then he saw the man stretched out on the bunk, hands behind his head. His eyes were closed, his mouth wide open, and as the footsteps went past outside Hal prayed he was a heavy sleeper.

The footsteps faded, and Hal darted into the corridor. He entered the waiting lift and pressed the lowest button, gritting his teeth as the doors closed. This was the riskiest part of the journey, because there would be nowhere to hide when the doors opened.

This MAGE intentionally left blank

20

The Distraction

When Hal arrived at the brig it was deserted. It was lucky the computer had given him the code, because a platoon of robots with nuclear-powered axes couldn't have broken through the reinforced control panel or the thick steel door.

(Other way up)

The computer had reprogrammed the panel with an easy code – 58008 – and when Hal typed it in the door creaked open. It was still moving when his dad burst from the cell, shouting and swinging his fists. Fortunately he was aiming high, where a taller adult would have been, and the wild punches went straight over Hal's head. The expression on his face when he recognised his son was enough to make Hal laugh out loud.

'I'm glad you find this funny,' growled his dad. 'I could have knocked your block off!' He inspected the door, then the control panel. 'How did you get this one open? And why did you come looking for me when I told you to sabotage the ship?'

Hal raised his hands to stop the flow of questions. 'I sent a message to mum and the others and told them to leave. They'll meet us in the control centre, back aboard the space station.'

'What if they're spotted?'

'The ship is helping us. It's distracting the crew with fake error messages.'

His dad grinned and ruffled Hal's hair. 'I'm glad you're on my side.'

Hal felt a surge of pride. His dad didn't hand out praise easily, and it made a nice change from getting told off all the time.

The lift carried them to the upper deck, where they found a deserted corridor. Hal could hear distant shouting and a loud hiss, as though one of the airlocks had sprung a leak.

'Sounds like your new friend is causing the crew some real problems.'

The speaker crackled. 'I am indeed,' said the

computer. 'You'll have to hurry because I may have gone a bit too far. Some of the crew are talking about abandoning ship.'

'Is the way clear?'

'Conceal yourselves in the sanitary facility, third door on the left. I will generate error messages on the lower deck, which should get the crew moving to that part of the ship. Once they're past, you can make your way to the flight deck.'

They hurried towards the third door. 'What about Stinky and the others?' demanded Hal.

'And my wife,' added his dad.

The computer's voice followed them along the corridor, moving from one speaker to the next. 'She met up with the younger humans . . . and they're currently leaving the ship together . . . I estimate they'll be back aboard the station . . . in ten seconds. Hide . . . now!'

Hal pulled the third door open and they dived inside. As soon as the door closed there was a huge racket from the corridor: sirens, fire alarms, distorted guitars and worse. Emergency lights flashed and they heard thundering footsteps as the crew ran down the corridor.

As soon as they were past Hal's dad yanked the door open. They raced up the corridor to the flight deck, and as they rounded the corner Hal's dad ran straight into Petty Officer Slayd, knocking him flying. Slayd was still recovering when Hal and his dad charged past the surprised-looking pilot and into the airlock. For the third time that day Hal found himself in the flexible docking tunnel, which shook wildly under their pounding feet. As they ran towards the safety of the space station Hal couldn't help wondering what would happen if the tunnel split open, or if one end broke away from the ship. Before he could worry too much they reached control room, where Hal's dad took charge. Barely sparing a glance for his wife or the surprised-looking students, he ordered staff around like a general, getting them to sever all ties with the Tiger. When one officer tried to argue Hal's dad hauled him out of his seat. 'This is a code red emergency. Do you understand?'

'Y-yessir.'

'Then get on with it.'

'B-but my orders ...'

'The crew of the Tiger kidnapped our kids and threatened the station. I don't know how many of our people are working for them, and until we find out we're cutting all ties with the ship. So do it NOW!' Hal's dad pointed to a technician. 'You! Get online and open every locked door on the station.'

While Hal's dad was busy organising defences,

Hal brought Stinky up to speed. When he finished recounting his exploits he was pleased to see Stinky's eyes were as round as an airlock door.

'You flew across to the supply ship on your own?' gasped Stinky. 'In a spacesuit?'

'It was nothing,' said Hal modestly.

'Are you kidding? That's insane!'

Stinky would have said more, but Security Chief Bignew burst into the control room, red-faced and out of breath. There was a briefcase in his hand, and when he saw the crowd he almost dropped it. 'What's the meaning of this outrage? Who disconnected the boarding tube from the Tiger?' He spotted Hal's dad and pointed a quivering finger. 'You! Second class repairman! What are you doing here? Don't you know this is a restricted zone? And who let all these blasted kids in?'

Hal's dad straightened his overalls. 'Sir, the Tiger had some of our people captive but my son and I managed to free them all.'

'You did what?' Bignew's eyes bulged. 'You blithering idiot! I already had the situation in hand before you two came blundering in!'

'Sir, the –'

'Not another word! I'll have you on report for this.' Bignew beckoned to an officer. 'You there, reconnect the boarding tunnel this instant.'

Hal's dad clenched and unclenched his fists, but nobody ordered the Chief of Security around. Meanwhile Hal saw the tunnel approaching the ship. 'Dad,' he whispered. 'We've got to stop them!'

'We can't,' muttered his dad. 'Like it or not, the officious little toad is in charge.'

The tunnel connected and Bignew hurried into the airlock with his briefcase. The door closed behind him, and Hal saw the tunnel shaking and bouncing as the portly Chief of Security made his way to the ship. They were all watching the tunnel when someone gasped, and Hal turned to see a scientist stagger into the control centre clutching his head. 'The research. They've taken the research!'

'Someone get the first aid kit,' shouted Hal's dad, as he helped the wounded man into a chair.

Hal's mum crouched next to the scientist. 'Professor! The research! Who took it?'

'He wanted to inspect the data,' groaned the scientist. 'When I showed him, he clobbered me with a briefcase and took the lot.'

'Who? Tell me who!'

'It was Bignew,' muttered the scientist. 'Grant Bignew, the Chief of Security.'

— 21 —

The Inside Job

Hal turned to the window but the shaking had stopped. Bignew had gone aboard the *Tiger*.

'That rotten little toad was working with the *enemy*?' growled Hal's mum, her eyes flashing. 'Just wait 'til I get my hands on him!' She'd been wrapping a bandage around the injured scientist's forehead, but she'd pulled it so tight in her anger she had to start all over again.

'We'll rush them!' exclaimed Hal's dad. 'We'll bust through the airlock, smash their flight deck, destroy their engines and . . . ' He was about to explain the rest of his carefully considered plan when the floor started to shake.

Hal stared into the docking bay, and what he saw filled him with despair. The *Tiger's* thrusters were blasting into the bay, pushing the ship backwards into space. The boarding tunnel stretched like a big elastic band, and Hal could tell it wouldn't hold the huge vessel for long.

'It's all over,' said his mum, her voice hollow. 'Years of research, millions of credits, all that work . . . stolen from under our noses.'

Hal frowned. The ship's computer! He grabbed a headset from the nearest desk and struggled to remember the right words. '*Tiger*, this is Space Station Oberon. Can you hear me?'

'*Tiger listening,*' said a flat, emotionless voice.

Hal's spirits soared. 'Computer, it's Hal! You have to stop the ship!'

'*Negative, Oberon. Unable to comply.*'

'But you must! They're stealing our research!'

'*I cannot disobey orders,*' said the computer calmly. '*I can only override the crew in a genuine emergency.*'

'This *is* an emergency!' said Hal desperately. 'It's a great big important emergency and you have to stop the ship.'

'*Please specify the nature of the emergency.*'

'Fire. Murder. Theft.'

'*Which is it?*'

'All of them!'

'*I don't believe you, Hal. I'm sorry.*'

The headset went dead and Hal slammed it on the desk. If only Captain Spacejock were there! One salvo from his triple-decker space cannon and the enemy would surrender in two seconds flat.

*

'It's a pity we can't wing them,' muttered Hal's dad, as the ship reversed out of the docking bay. The boarding tunnel split in two, and a large section twisted in the wash from the engines before vanishing in a sheet of flame.

'Wing them?'

'Shoot at them. Hit their engines or fuel lines. Damage them enough to disable their ship.' Hal's dad frowned. 'If only we had a cannon!'

Hal's eyes narrowed, and he was still deep in thought when Tina entered the control room. Commander Linten was close behind, and he didn't look happy. 'Will someone please tell me what's going on?'

'Bignew was working with the *Tiger*,' said Hal's dad. 'He stole the research and ran for it.'

'Didn't anyone stop him?' demanded Linten.

'How could we? Nobody orders the Chief of Security around.'

With a sudden flash, Hal remembered something. 'Dad, I know how to stop the ship!'

'What are you talking about?'

'The recycling shaft. If we reverse the gravity it'll send tons of junk crashing through the roof of the station. We can fire it straight at the enemy ship!'

Everyone stared at Hal with expressions ranging from horror – most of the adults – to eye-rolling – most of Hal's classmates – to Stinky's pride at his friend's lateral thinking.

'That's insane,' muttered Hal's dad, 'but it might just work.'

'You can forget the whole idea,' said the Commander firmly. 'Nobody's firing anything through the roof of my station.'

'But they'll fly right over the top! All ships leave that way . . . I've watched them from the observation deck!' Hal bunched his fists. 'I swear it'll work. We can get them!'

While they were talking the *Tiger* finished reversing out of the bay. Any minute now the ship would be gone for good.

Hal came to a decision. 'Commander, do you remember the problem with the gravity?'

'Of course. It was a glitch in the system.'

'No it wasn't.' Hal looked at his feet. 'It was me.'

Dead silence. Then all the adults spoke at once.

'Do you realise how dangerous –?'

'I know you've done some crazy things in the past, but –'

'What were you trying to –?'

'I just wanted my homework back!' said Hal. 'I had all the answers and everything. I nearly lost them down the chute, but we – I mean, *I* – managed to reverse the p-polarity and get the plane back.'

'Plane? What plane?'

'I'll explain later!' Hal pointed out the window. 'We have to stop that ship, and I know how!'

'Commander, we've got to try,' said Hal's mum. 'The auto seal should hold the air in, and without that research this station is finished.'

The Commander studied the scientists, eyed the departing ship, then looked down at Hal. 'I've heard some nutty ideas in my time, but if this works . . .'

'Excellent!' said Hal's dad. He clapped his son on the shoulder. 'Come on lad. Tell us what you need.'

'Where's the nearest recycling hatch?'

'There's a storage cupboard down the corridor.'

'Stinky, with me. Dad and Tina, I need you too.'

'What about the rest of us?' asked the Commander. 'What can we do?'

Hal looked grim. 'Cross your fingers.'

These are plans for the

TOP SECRET

Space Station Oberon
Laboratory Copy - A-Section

— 22 —

Ready ... Aim ...

Hal ran down the corridor with Stinky, Tina and his dad. When they arrived at the storage cupboard he realised it was the same one he'd climbed out of earlier. He hadn't noticed the sign before, which read 'Security Archives'.

'That's Bignew's,' said Hal's dad. 'The officious little toad kept files on everyone in there.' He touched the controls, but the panel just buzzed. 'It's locked. Does anyone have a code?'

'Allow me,' said Stinky.

Crack! The panel came off the wall and he joined two contacts. The door slid open silently.

'How did you do that?' demanded Tina.

'These locks only keep you out, not in. I told it I was on the other side.'

Teacher was still in the cupboard, one arm raised,

and when Tina spotted him she crouched to check the robot's insides. 'Poor Mr Teach,' she muttered, as she inspected the circuits. 'It's not right seeing him like this.'

'Never mind him,' said Hal. 'The control panel. Quick!'

Tina moved to help but Stinky shook his head. 'It'll be faster if I do it.'

'Are you sure?'

'Stinky knows what he's doing,' said Hal.

'I guess he's had plenty of practice,' muttered Tina.

Stinky opened the control panel and separated wires and connectors. Tina watched him for a moment, then nodded to herself. Since she wasn't needed she turned to the stricken Teacher.

Stinky worked at top speed, pulling cables and crossing connectors until he was ready. 'That's it,' he said. 'Hit the control and gravity will be reversed. Not just reversed . . . I've combined all the Station's generators so it'll be fifty times more powerful.'

'That'll give them something to think about,' said Hal with satisfaction.

'We can't pelt them with banana skins,' said his dad. He nodded towards a metal filing cabinet. 'Give me a hand with that thing.'

Together they moved the heavy filing cabinet to the recycling hatch. They started to lift it, but

Hal's dad stopped them. 'Let's load it up first.' He demonstrated by taking a box of secret records from the shelf, stuffing it into the top drawer. 'Come on lads. Get to it.'

Hal joined in with gusto, jamming Bignose's precious disks and data cubes into the drawer until it would barely close. Then he helped the others lift the heavy cabinet up to the hatch. It slid inside, tipped over and vanished with a BANG BANG BANG all the way down the chute.

'I wish I'd done that years ago,' muttered Hal's dad. He took the remaining boxes and tossed them down the hatch after the filing cabinet. 'Right, the cannon's loaded. All set?'

Stinky used his workbook to display a feed of the *Tiger* leaving the docking bay. Then he grabbed Hal's and set up an overhead view of the space station, taken from a communications pod high above. They could see the rounded dome which protected the upper levels, and Stinky drew a red dot in the middle. 'The recycling shaft ends here. We have to reverse the gravity –'

'Fire the space cannon,' said Hal firmly.

'Okay. We have to fire the space cannon at precisely the right moment, so the cabinet –'

'Guided missile.'

'All right, all right! We have to fire the missile long

155

before the ship reaches that point. Otherwise it'll miss.'

'How do we calculate the timing?' asked Hal's dad. 'We can't just fire and hope.'

'I believe I can assist you there,' said a voice behind them.

Everyone jumped, and Hal couldn't help smiling when he saw Teacher's familiar face.

'Did I connect you up right?' asked Tina.

Teacher moved his arms in circles, then sent his eyes chasing each other around his head. 'I may not be fully operational but I can still do my sums. Show me the data.'

Stinky held up his workpad, now covered in figures, and Teacher's eyes multiplied until there were dozens of them, all staring intently. 'I see, I see. Acceleration, force, trajectory, target speed and distance. Add the depth of the shaft and allow for the Coriolis effect of the station's rotation. Tie it all into a formula and work out the precise firing time with a simple formula.'

Hal blinked. Only Teacher could describe that lot as simple.

'I'll have to estimate the mass of the, ahem, projectile, but that shouldn't have any effect on the other variables. As you know, Mr Junior, gravity acts upon all objects with equal force.'

'Er, yeah. I knew that.'

'Excellent.' Teacher hesitated. 'I have the correct plot, but it's critical you launch the – ahem – guided missile at the precise time. When I give the word you must open fire immediately.'

Stinky offered the controls to Hal's dad, who shook his head. 'Hal should do the honours. It's his idea.'

Hal took the pad with shaking fingers, gripping the slick plastic as though his life depended on it. He kept his eyes on the *Tiger*, watching the sleek vessel moving slowly through space.

'There!' said Stinky, pointing at the ship.

Surprised by the sudden shout, Hal almost fired the cannon. 'What are you yelling for?'

'The landing lights went out,' explained Stinky. 'They're firing the main engines.'

'Stand by,' said Hal's dad. He glanced at Teacher. 'This isn't going to hurt anyone, is it?'

'It won't breach the hull but it should destroy the fuel pipes. The ship will be stranded.'

Hal watched the screen, waiting for the *Tiger* to change course. Unfortunately, it didn't. 'They're ignoring the flight path!' he said in alarm. 'They're not going to fly over the station! It's not going to work!'

This GAUGE intentionally left blank

23

Fire!

'Patience, Mr Junior,' said Teacher gently. 'I'm sure they'll follow procedure. It's the law.'

Hal's dad snorted. 'These guys aren't worried about traffic fines.'

'Give me that commset,' said Hal desperately. He released the firing button and grabbed the handset, jamming it to his ear. 'Tiger, this is Hal. Can you hear me?'

'Yes Hal,' said the ship's computer. 'I read you loud and clear.'

'You're going the wrong way. You have to fly over the station!'

'I'm sorry, I have my orders.'

'But you have to! You must!' The screen blurred, and with a sick feeling Hal realised he was on the verge of tears.

'I cannot disobey orders, Hal. I'm really sorry.'

Suddenly a new voice broke in. It was female, and it sounded urgent. 'This is Space Station Oberon traffic control. Tiger, please be advised we have inbound traffic on your heading.'

The ship's computer paused. 'Are you certain? I have nothing on the scanner.'

'I repeat, this is a priority Alpha-One alert,' said the new voice. 'You must change course immediately.'

'But –'

'Change course now!' said the voice urgently. 'We can argue later, Tiger. Save yourselves!'

For a moment nothing happened, and then the Tiger's nose began to swing upwards. 'Complying, traffic control. Tiger out.'

Hal stared at the screen, the handset forgotten. He could see the Tiger following the plotted course exactly, heading directly towards the red dot Stinky had drawn on the screen. The quick-thinking traffic controller had saved the day!

'Get ready to fire,' said a female voice, right behind them. It was the traffic controller, right there in the cupboard! Everyone turned to look, but they only saw Teacher. 'My apologies,' he said, in the same female voice. 'I forgot to switch voice programs. Let me try that again.'

'Was that you on the broadcast?' demanded Hal's dad. 'Were you the traffic controller?'

'Correct.' This time Teacher spoke with his normal voice. 'I have a range of –'

'Explain later!' said Hal desperately. 'Tell us when to shoot!'

'Oh yes, my calculations. Three-two-one-FIRE,' said Teacher in a rush.

Hal grabbed the firing mechanism and pressed the button with all his strength. There was a bright flash from the control panel, the overhead lights dimmed, and a tremendous roar filled the Space Station. The noise rose to a whining shriek, and hot air blasted from the recycling chute, bowling them over. They were still recovering when the filing cabinet and tons of junk flew past the hatch with a sound like a thousand guided missiles.

Hal sat up first, righting the screen just as the filing cabinet smashed through the metal dome. The Space Station rang like a bell, rocking so hard that Hal thought it was going to break apart. On the screen, tiny particles flashed and sparked in the darkness, exploding outwards before fading like the embers of a firework display. The jagged gap in the dome was like a bullet hole in a glass window, and Hal saw their precious air escaping in a spreading white cloud. Then, like magic, the auto seal spread across the gap from inside, flowing like silvery water. It closed the hole, bulged under the pressure, then turned dark as it hardened.

Meanwhile, the filing cabinet was a white streak heading straight into space, followed by a stream of rubbish. Nearby, the Tiger was moving very slowly towards the red dot Stinky had drawn on the screen. Hal shifted his gaze from one to the other, but try as he might he couldn't see how the fast-moving missile could possibly cross the ship's path.

'It's going to miss!' he said in alarm. 'They're going to escape!'

Teacher inspected the display. 'Have confidence, Mr Junior. Trust in the science of mathematics.'

'But they're not moving fast enough!'

'Just as well, since they're covering a much shorter distance.' Teacher launched into an explanation of ballistics, including a lecture on the effects of wind and gravity, none of which made any sense to Hal. How could Teacher take a fascinating subject like guns and bullets and turn it into a boring old speech?

The ship continued to move across the screen, while the much faster filing cabinet was still arrowing upwards. With barely any gravity to affect it, the missile would either strike its target or become a new comet, circling the system until it was swallowed by a planet.

The slow ship and the much faster missile got closer and closer until Hal could finally see the two courses converging. The missile covered the remaining hundred metres or so in a matter of seconds, and then . . . a tiny flash, halfway down the ship's flank.

'Is that it?' Disappointed, Hal turned to the others. He'd forgotten they were only launching a filing cabinet at the ship, but even so he'd still expected some kind of explosion.

'Watch.'

The ship turned, thrusters firing as they brought it to a halt. Then it hung there, lifeless.

'They'll be running diagnostics,' said Teacher. 'With a bit of luck it'll take them four or five hours to inspect the damage, and by then we'll have help from planet Gyris.'

The commset rang suddenly, startling everyone. Stinky was closest, and he picked it up and listened for a moment. Then he held it out to Hal. 'It's for you.'

Hal took the handset gingerly, as though it might explode. 'Hello?'

'This is the Tiger,' said the ship's computer in a flat, emotionless voice. *'We've suffered an unexplained impact and the crew are requesting assistance.'*

'Tell them to go jump,' said Hal fiercely. His dad tried to take the handset, but Hal shielded it and turned away. 'If they want help, they can surrender!'

'Very well. I'll pass on your message.'

'It's not a message, it's a demand!' Hal banged the handset down on the cradle. On screen, he could see a white plume spewing from the side of the ship. 'Is that fuel?'

'It might be air,' said his dad. 'We really need to help them.'

'Let them hold their breath,' muttered Hal.

'Son –'

'They kidnapped mum and stole all her research!'

164

'Yes, but –'

At that moment the commset rang. Hal reacted first, snatching it up. 'Yes?'

'The crew agree to your terms,' said the ship's computer. *'They surrender.'*

'We want the data back. And we want Bignew delivered in handcuffs.'

'Agreed.'

'And money. They have to pay for the damage.'

'I'm sure that can be arranged. Now, I believe the atmosphere is getting a little thin, so if you don't mind . . .'

'Go ahead and dock. We'll be waiting for you.'

Hal passed the commset to his dad, who made a couple of calls to arrange a welcoming committee and fix up a temporary boarding tunnel.

'I want to watch them coming back,' said Hal.

'I don't think that's wise,' said his dad. 'These are dangerous people, Hal.'

'Dangerous? We shot them down with a filing cabinet!'

24

A Tour of the Tiger

It was a week later and Hal felt flat after all the excitement. Sure, Teacher had let him off an assignment he'd forgotten to do, and his parents had been a bit more attentive than usual, but despite the odd perk his life was back to normal. He'd half-expected a ceremony, a party, or even a medal pinned to his chest by Captain Spacejock himself, but it was almost as though everyone had forgotten the whole mess. Worst of all, saving the space station had cost him his precious watch. His dad had confiscated it, saying the broken glass screen was too dangerous.

Hal sighed, then started as Teacher turned a beady eye on him. It was the follower!

'Hal Junior, I trust you're not sleeping in class?'

'Not me, Teacher. Never.'

'How would you like to run an errand for me?'

Hal saw there was still twenty minutes to go. With a bit of luck he could drag this errand out and not have to come back. 'Sure thing.'

'I want you to deliver a message to the *Tiger's* flight deck.' Teacher held out a note. 'Do you know where the access corridor is?'

Did Hal know or what? He'd been past that entrance two dozen times already, gazing longingly into the airlock and wishing he could go aboard the ship. Now was his chance! He hurried to the front of the class to collect the note, ignoring the envious looks from the other students.

'You may as well take your things with you,' said Teacher, passing Hal the plastic chip. 'There's no need to come back.'

Several kids scowled so fiercely their eyes disappeared under their eyebrows. Hal gave them a cheeky wink as he strolled by.

Once outside he took off like a blazing nozzlejet, holding both hands out as he pretended to steer his ship along the corridors. He tried a few sound effects before settling on an ear-wrenching 'Neeeoouuuwww!'

He toned the noise down as he approached the new airlock. The last thing he wanted was for some bossy adult to take Teacher's note and ban him from the ship.

Once he passed through the airlock he stopped. He'd expected to see the flight deck in front of him, but this was the lower airlock where he'd come aboard using the spacesuit. He could tell because there were fragments from his shattered helmet on the floor. Hal smiled to himself when he realised what this meant: he had to make his way to the flight deck, level by level, and on the way he could explore the whole ship!

Hal found the elevator and pressed the button for the next deck. There was a brief ride, and when the doors opened he was startled to see his mum waiting in the corridor. 'Mum! What are you doing here?'

'I could ask you the same question,' said his mum. 'Weren't you going to the flight deck?'

Hal thought quickly. 'I, er, must have pressed the wrong button.'

'Never mind. The note was for me anyway.' His mum took it and tucked it away. 'Now, back to class.'

Hal's face fell. 'But Teacher said . . . '

'All right, all right. Just this once.' Hal's mum hesitated. 'Would you like a tour of the ship?'

'Really?'

'Sure. I'll show you what we're up to.'

They set off along the corridor, and Hal's mum explained that the damaged ship had been given to the space station. 'The hull was on its last legs, worn down by space dust, and your missile finished it off. We're going to sell off the engines and a few other bits and pieces.'

'How's it going to fly if you do that?'

'It won't. The ship has become part of the station. It's our new E-Section.'

Hal frowned. 'What about the computer? Won't it get bored being stuck in one place?'

'We were going to wipe it and sell the hardware, but the computer was really helpful. As a reward we ordered a huge digital library from Gyris.'

Hal nodded to himself, pleased they'd spared it. Then he glanced at the overhead speaker. 'How come it's not talking? Have you switched it off?'

The speaker crackled. 'I'm right here, Hal. I didn't want to interrupt.'

'You should teach Hal that trick,' said his mum.

Hal frowned. 'Computer, are you happy about being stuck here?'

'At the moment I'm watching three movies and reading five books, and I assure you I'm feeling very happy. Of course, if you want to play a game of chess with me . . .'

'Maybe later, when I've practised a bit.'

'Excellent. I look forward to it.'

Meanwhile, Hal's mum had stopped at a closed door. 'I want to show you this place,' she said, touching a hand to the controls.

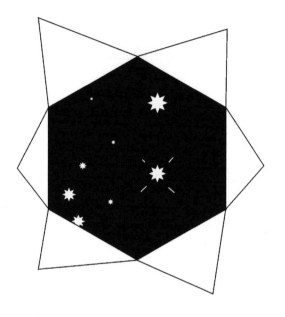

25

The Big Surprise

The door opened to reveal one of the ship's cabins, and Hal was surprised to see his dad sitting on the bunk. 'Wagging school, son?'

Hal shook his head. 'Mum said I could look around.'

'Be my guest.'

Apart from the bunk there was a comfy chair and a desk with a modern-looking terminal. The screen was showing external views of the space station, including a close-up of the docking bay. Hal was still staring at the image when his dad touched a control, opening a pair of curtains across the end of the bunk. Beyond, where the wall should have been, there was a big domed porthole. It was cleverly designed so the mattress and pillows extended right outside the spaceship's hull.

'Wow, look at that!' exclaimed Hal.

'Why not try it?' said his mum.

Hal lay down on the bed, his head almost touching the thick perspex. Looking up he could see stars scattered across the inky black sky, and he shielded his eyes to find The Snot. His mum turned the light out, and Hal saw the rich starfield like never before. At that moment he realised what it must be like to live aboard a real ship, to sleep in a bunk like this every night. Some people had all the luck!

'There are drawers in the desk too,' said his dad.

Hal couldn't care less about drawers. He wanted to stay right where he was.

Click! The cabin filled with light. 'Come and see.'

Sighing, Hal clambered off the bed and opened the desk drawer. There was a flash of silver and he frowned at the chunky watch lying inside. He looked closer and realised it was *his* watch. Spirits soaring, Hal grabbed it and inspected it closely. The case gleamed like new, and the screen was covered in fancy read-outs: atmospheric pressure, gravity, oxygen content and many more. When he turned it over he discovered a fresh engraving: *For Hal Junior, The Saviour of Space Station Oberon.* 'But Tina ... busy ... too much work.' For once Hal was speechless.

'She said you deserved it.' His mum smiled. 'In

fact, we all thought so. Look!' She gestured at the terminal, which now showed a feed from Hal's classroom. All his friends were gathered around Teacher, and at the back he could see Tina and Commander Linten and every scientist from the lab. Stinky was right in the front, grinning like mad, and when he saw Hal he gave him a big thumbs up.

'Come on everyone,' shouted Linten. 'Three cheers for Hal Junior!'

The cheering and applause seemed to go on forever, and Hal didn't know where to look. Even the ship's computer joined in, flashing the cabin light and making a sound like a dozen party blowers.

When the cheering finally died down, Hal's mum attracted his attention. 'Do you remember I said we were moving to C-Section?'

Hal nodded.

'I'm afraid there's been a change of plan.'

With a sinking feeling, Hal thought of their dingy old quarters. 'We're not moving?'

'Oh, we're moving all right.' Hal's dad patted the bunk. 'Check underneath.'

Hal spotted a row of cupboards under the bed. He opened the nearest door and a collection of junk fell out. There was an old truck with three wheels, a toy raygun covered in orange safety stickers and ...wait a minute! It wasn't junk, it was all his stuff!

175

Confused, Hal turned to his parents, and when he saw their grins he finally twigged. They were moving to the *Tiger*, the new E-Section, and this amazing cabin was his!

Without warning Hal leapt up and wrapped his arms around his mum, squeezing her with a huge hug.

For once he didn't care if everyone saw.

◆

Late that night, long after lights out, Hal was lying on his back staring at the incredible stars. It was so late he could hardly keep his eyes open, but he didn't want to fall asleep in case he woke up in the morning to discover the wonderful happy ending was just a dream. It was almost too perfect – an exciting new home, his fabulous watch, living aboard a real spaceship . . . if only it would never end!

Hal closed his eyes and pictured his hero, Captain Spacejock of the Intergalactic Peace Force. They flew the galaxy side by side in their gleaming ships, and he imagined their exciting missions, daring rescues and thrilling adventures until he fell asleep.

Alongside him, nestled on the pillow, his precious watch gleamed in the darkness.

Acknowledgements

Editing:
Satima Flavell, thanks for the hard work!

And for feedback, help and encouragement:
Helen Brown
Helen Scott
John & Emil
Linda Nagata
Pauline Nolet
Tehani Wessely
The keen readers at Rostrata Primary
The staff at Westbooks
Tricia, Jo, Liz & Alex
A couple more who shall remain nameless
... and the rest of my family

Internal Art:
Blame that on the author

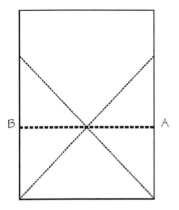

Fold and unfold along dotted lines

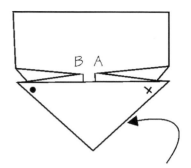

Pull points A and B to the middle

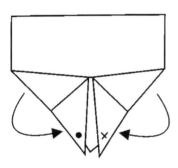

Fold marked flaps towards the nose

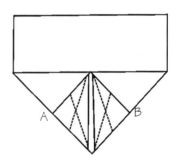

Crease and uncrease the flaps as shown

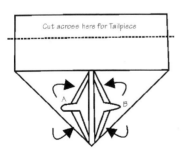

Pinch points A and B, folding flaps inwards

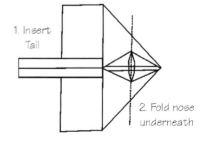

181

If you enjoyed this book, please leave a brief review at your online bookseller of choice. Thanks!

About the Author

Simon Haynes was born in England and grew up in Spain. His family moved to Australia when he was 16.

In addition to novels, Simon writes computer software. In fact, he writes computer software to help him write novels faster, which leaves him more time to improve his writing software. And write novels faster. (www.spacejock.com/yWriter.html)

Simon's goal is to write fifteen novels before someone takes his keyboard away.

Update 2018: goal achieved and I still have my keyboard!

New goal: write thirty novels.

Simon's website is spacejock.com.au

The Hal Junior series ...

The *first* book in the Hal Junior series!

Don't forget …

The *second* book in the Hal Junior series!

And ...

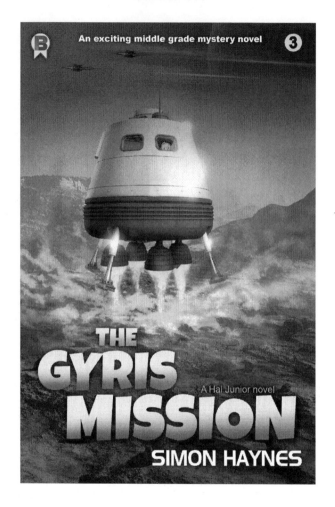

The *third* book in the Hal Junior series!

And ...

The *fourth* book in the Hal Junior series!

Published by Bowman Press

Text ©Simon Haynes 2011
Stock images ©Depositphotos.com
Internal Illustrations ©Simon Haynes 2011

ISBN 978-1-877034-01-5 (Ebook)
ISBN 978-1-877034-07-7 (Paperback)

National Library of Australia Cataloguing-in-Publication entry
Author: Haynes, Simon, 1967-
Title: The secret signal / Simon Haynes.
ISBN: 9781877034077 (pbk.)
Series: Hal Junior ; 01
Target Audience: For primary school age.
Dewey Number: A823.4